"What's your hurry, Ace?"

Heidi laughed nervously—a sound that couldn't belong to her, the mighty Heidi Malone.

"You're right." Ben lifted one—only one—hand from her shoulder. "What's the hurry? It's not like I've been waiting fifteen damn years."

"You have?" she said, her voice ingenuously soft. "You've been waiting for me?"

"Call it a fantasy, but yeah." He reached for a sprig of hair that had escaped her baseball cap and twirled it around his finger. "I've been waiting for you."

"I'm your fantasy?" She reached up and touched his face, and the hair that had fallen loose on his brow. "I don't think I've been anyone's fantasy before."

Ben's eyes slowly closed, slowly opened. His mouth pulled into a regretful smile. "You were everyone's fantasy, Heidi. Didn't you know that?"

"You've got to be kidding," she said, and frowned at his statement. Her mood had shifted, taking on a hint of perturbation. They weren't even in a relationship and she already had a headache. Not a good sign.

"Wrong. I'm dead serious." He pulled her closer and she knew from the look in his eyes that he intended to prove it.

Dear Reader,

Harlequin Temptation celebrates its fifteenth birthday this year! When we launched in 1984, our goal was to be the most sensual, most contemporary series in the marketplace. Today we're still that—and *more*. Each month we bring you four fun sexy stories that range from romantic fantasy to "Blazing" sensuality. Temptation is *the* series for women of the new millennium.

Over the years popular authors such as Jayne Ann Krentz, Barbara Delinsky, LaVyrle Spencer and Carla Neggers have contributed to the success of Temptation. Many of our writers have gone on to achieve fame and fortune—and the *New York Times* bestseller list!

In celebration of our fifteen years, I'm delighted to introduce you to three shining stars. Say hello to Pamela Burford, Alison Kent and Donna Sterling who are each thrilled to bring you their sizzling stories in September, October and November.

I hope you enjoy these talented authors, as I hope you will enjoy all the fabulous books and authors to come.

Happy Reading!

Birgit Davis-Todd
Senior Editor, Harlequin Books

P.S. We love to hear from readers! Write and tell us what your favorite Temptation book was over the past fifteen years. We'll publish a list of the top fifty!

Harlequin Books
225 Duncan Mill Road
Don Mills, Ontario
CANADA M3B 3K9

FOUR MEN
& A LADY
Alison Kent

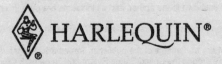

TORONTO • NEW YORK • LONDON
AMSTERDAM • PARIS • SYDNEY • HAMBURG
STOCKHOLM • ATHENS • TOKYO • MILAN • MADRID
PRAGUE • WARSAW • BUDAPEST • AUCKLAND

I owe a big thanks to the following people.

Temptation author Julie Elizabeth Leto, for vetting my
cultural references. Sam Houston State University Bearkat
Joe Holloway, for advising me on the band.
Albany High School, Albany, Oregon, 1984 graduate,
Paul Williams, my brother the rock star, for grounding me
in the times. You've all made me feel very old! And I'm not!

To the Rocks of Gibraltar in the muddy terrain
of my sea. Walt and Jan.

This one is for Susan Sheppard,
after whom I'd name my firstborn.
If he wasn't twenty. And male.
So, instead, I'll name my star.

ISBN 0-373-25850-X

FOUR MEN & A LADY

Visit us at www.romance.net

Printed in U.S.A.

Dear Reader,

It's Harlequin Temptation's fifteenth anniversary. Where has the time gone? When this sexy series was born fifteen years ago, I wasn't even as old as the *Four Men & a Lady* whose story you're about to read.

As young as I was, however, I was old enough to appreciate Temptation's boldly sensuous stories. And when I think about the current *New York Times* bestselling authors who launched the line and the future *New York Times* bestsellers bringing readers the red-hot love stories of today, well, no wonder Temptation is such a blazing success.

I'm honored to write for the line and especially thrilled to be a part of this anniversary celebration. Here's to the next fifteen years. And the fifteen after that.

You can write to me in care of Harlequin Enterprises, 225 Duncan Mill Road, Don Mills, Ontario, Canada M3B 3K9. Or you can visit Harlequin Temptation at http://www.romance.net and find me via the link to my personal page.

Best wishes!

Alison Kent

Books by Alison Kent

HARLEQUIN TEMPTATION
594—CALL ME
623—THE HEARTBREAK KID
664—THE GRINCH MAKES GOOD
741—THE BADGE AND THE BABY

Prologue

RUBBING AT THE SCAR along the curve of his jawline was a bad habit Ben Tannen had never been able to break.

He caught himself in the act too often while driving. Or when lost in thought. The worst was when he was lost in thought while driving.

Like now.

He glanced in his rearview mirror at the Southwest Texas setting-sun streaks of turquoise and orange-yellow, and found his thumb working the groove that began center-chin and ran to the midpoint of his ear.

An inch higher and she might've put out his eye. Or so the doctors had said. And wouldn't that have been a parent's dire prediction come true.

Ben knew the diagnosis wasn't entirely accurate. The strength of Heidi's fury, her hurt and humiliation, had far surpassed the strength of her swing.

Still, the gash had been bad enough. The chain Heidi used to lock up her bike was old, had lost most of its blue plastic sheathing and hadn't been kind to his face.

She'd acted in the heat of the moment. Had she stopped to think, she'd've realized the end with the combination lock had a lot more potential as a weapon.

He did have that to be thankful for.

The pain had lingered longer than he'd admitted during any of the endless medical follow-ups or reconstructive consultations his parents had forced him to attend.

Even now he swore he still felt an occasional twinge. Like the skin and bone had intentionally enclosed the pain of the injury so he'd understand the consequences of making an ass of himself.

He understood all right. The consequences were there every morning when he looked in the mirror to shave. He had a hell of a scar reminding him to keep his nose and his jaw and even his checkbook where they belonged.

He also understood any feeling that remained was only in his mind...and only when his thoughts drifted to Heidi. He steered clear of her direction, as a rule.

After scraping his face off an asphalt parking lot, a guy'd have to be a moron to go back for more. Which Ben had. Three times.

So sue him if he'd been both an ass and a moron. He bet there wouldn't be one person at this weekend's high school reunion who didn't have a closet full of skeletal remains.

Even the Mighty Heidi Malone had old tales to tell.

Ben forced his hand from his face.

He wasn't surprised she'd done as well for herself as she had, or that the press had bestowed on her the epithet after she'd won a particularly high-profile case.

She'd had amazing success as a woman defending women in matters of sex and race. She'd come a long way, baby.

A living breathing cliché, Heidi'd been the girl

from the wrong side of the tracks forced by a jagged turn in a county line to attend school with the sons and daughters of class and privilege.

She'd also been the only female in Sherwood Grove, Texas' Johnson High School's award-winning jazz quintet. Heidi'd played alto sax like nobody's business and tolerated no less from the other four teen musicians.

After a particularly bad night of practice not long into their freshman year, in fact, she'd christened their group of five The Deck, accusing the rest of them of playing as flat as a bunch of personality-impaired face cards.

Her tirade had dissolved into a fit of giggles and bathroom jokes about royal flushes, and the five had left that evening with nicknames none had managed to shake over the next four years.

Heidi'd labeled herself The Joker and Ben—The Ace—had had a hard time keeping silent. She didn't seem to realize she'd chosen a card that had no real place in the deck.

He wondered if Heidi would even make it to this weekend's reunion. Jack had assured Ben that she'd responded to the invitation, though it had been very last-minute. And very tentative. Like that was any kind of surprise.

Heidi'd never been much for convention. Come hell or high water she'd been determined to make her own way in the world...as he'd learned there beside the bicycle racks on their final day as high school seniors.

Leaving the parking lot of the Stonebridge Reporter, Ben turned on the headlights and turned off the memories. Forty minutes and he'd be in Austin.

He hoped Heidi showed tonight. He really did. Tonight had been fifteen years in the making. And he was ready.

He patted his slacks pocket, smiled at the folded square of old paper there. Yep. It was time to see if Mighty Heidi was as good as her word.

Sure she'd paid off her monetary debt, but that wasn't all she'd promised him those many years ago. He had every intention of collecting her IOU.

She'd made a mistake when she'd skinned him alive with that cutting tongue of hers. Because now he was her skeleton. And he was coming out of her closet.

1

THE LIGHTS WERE DIM, the air was smoky and the music was loud nineties rock.

The door to The Cave Down Below closed behind her, and Heidi stopped in the entryway to get her bearings. The club occupied a lot of space on the first floor of the old warehouse, but it only took her a minute to see what there was to see.

Dance floor and stage on the left. Bar at the rear. Pool tables, video games, big-screen TVs to the right.

A gust of wind tickled her short hem. She glanced back briefly at the hugging, giggling couple elbowing their way through the door.

They jostled her, apologized and continued inside. Having loitered long enough—she certainly wouldn't call the delay avoidance—she followed the man and woman into the club.

And was immediately assaulted by the noise.

The clatter of air hockey disks and pool balls competed with the bells and whistles, tsssbooms and thuds, whomps and rrrooaars of video games and pinball machines.

People mingled from the doorway of the club to the opposite end which looked half a football field away. Voices raised above the chaos to shout drink orders and roar "Over here!" and laugh belly deep.

The pulse of humanity. A living breathing collective consciousness that rose and fell with a heartbeat's deep rhythm. Heidi released a sigh along with the last of a ridiculous case of nerves. Walking inside wasn't the step through the looking glass she'd been expecting.

The Cave was no different than the few clubs she frequented in Dallas when letting down her hair with Georgia. Often the places she and her partner took clients to celebrate the court's decisions toed this same sort of rowdy line.

But she was definitely overdressed. Or underdressed, judging by the looks lingering on the hem of her short black dress. Obviously her idea of casual involved more bare skin than the regulars at The Cave were used to seeing.

Oh, well. She'd dressed to party, to play, to have fun. She'd also dressed to kill and to vamp—in case the need for either arose. So far, neither had.

She hadn't seen a single sign of Ben.

Ben Tannen. Amazing, wasn't it, that two words, a simple name, could so easily return a grown woman to the days of adolescent angst?

Here she was, her heart beating like she was sixteen. The shiver of anticipation zigging down her spine, the beads of perspiration zagging between her breasts, couldn't have been more real.

And all over a boy, now a man, who'd never acknowledged her teenage crush.

Heidi shook her head. *Enough silliness,* she vowed, returning her attention to the crowd. Not only had she seen no sign of Ben, but Randy, Jack and Quentin seemed absent, as well. In fact, she'd seen only one or two vaguely familiar faces.

The lack of recognition would've made for one of those classically uncomfortable reunion moments had either classmate approached. Neither did. Which surprised Heidi not in the least.

She expected many such non-moments this weekend. After all, she could hardly be recognized now when fifteen years ago she'd been virtually invisible. A nobody in the consummate sense of the word.

Making her way to the bar through the crush of bodies, she ordered a beer and eased onto the bare edge of a bar stool. Legs crossed, she swiveled to the side and glanced out at the crowd. One face after another came into focus, the details fell into place.

There was Starr, the head cheerleader who'd dated Ronnie the quarterback and been eight weeks pregnant at graduation. She appeared to be at least eight months pregnant now. As Heidi looked on, Ronnie pushed away from the crowded table, leaned down to give Starr a peck on the cheek then went to join friends at the bank of pinball machines. Heidi smiled when she realized the ex-quarterback's rounded belly mirrored his wife's.

Her gaze picked up another couple. Eric and Ellen, the twins, valedictorian and salutatorian respectively. They'd been so competitive, both academically and personally, that neither had a life outside their studies. Neither wore a wedding band now. Heidi couldn't help but wonder about the price of their success. Or of her own.

Dang it, she was sounding like Georgia. Georgia Banks was a natural-born litigator and Heidi was

pleased to call the stunning black woman both partner and best friend. But she really needed to find a
new voice for her conscience.

One that wasn't so disconcertingly accurate in her
summation of Heidi's obsession with one particular
man. A man who obviously couldn't pry the silver
spoon from his mouth long enough to down a cold
one with old friends. Or old enemies.

Heidi continued to visually canvas the room. She
took in the looks slanted her way, not so terribly different from the looks of years ago. They were still trying to figure her out. Who she was. Where she came
from. Whether or not she belonged.

She sighed. Conscience or not, a dose of Georgia's
irreverent humor would certainly spice up what
looked to be a long night ahead. Which meant a long
day tomorrow. And Sunday as well.

One thing was certain. Next time Heidi was in high
school, she would work a little harder to avoid earn-
ing the very title she found herself wearing—Most
Likely Fifteenth Class Reunion Wallflower. Silently
laughing, she lifted her cold longneck—only to have
the bottle snatched from her hand.

"Hey!" she cried, looking up and over her shoulder
and into the face of... "Quentin Marks!"

"Heidi Malone. Long time no see. Long time no
speak to. Long time no hear from." Quentin winked
and downed a quarter of her beer, watching her face
as he swallowed. His eyes twinkled with that endear-
ing Marks mischief. His mouth turned up in that
quirky Marks grin. "I see you've descended from
your throne to consort with the commoners."

She knew she was smiling like a fool, but it was so

good to see what the years had made of the boy who had been one of her very best friends. "Since when does The Joker sit on a throne? I was the one with the silly clothes and goofy hat, remember."

"Goofy hat, right. I wondered what that mess was up there on your head." Quentin patted the hair she'd let grow from the bleached-out, straggly waif cut of her high school days to the full-bodied mass of curls she'd let loose for the night. "I knew it couldn't be hair. If it was hair, then you couldn't be Heidi. You are Heidi, aren't you?"

"Quentin, you goof." Unable to contain herself a minute longer, she flung both arms around Quentin's neck and hugged him, nearly losing her seat on the stool as she did.

Quentin heartily returned the embrace, his broad hands securing her balance before he pulled back to take another look and another feel of her hair. "This is great, even though you did wear the butchered look well."

She stuck out her tongue and scooted more securely onto her seat, tugging her hem down her thighs. "After all that chopping I did, I wasn't sure it would ever grow out."

"It grew out. It grew curly. And—" he caught a strand around one finger "—it grew into a different color."

Weren't chemicals and coloring a girl's best friend? "You might want to keep your nose out of my hairdresser's business unless you want him to take a pair of scissors to that horse's tail hanging down your neck."

"Think again, Delilah," Quentin said and tossed

his head like an arrogant thoroughbred. "You're looking at five years' worth of work here. Besides, if the recording industry takes a dive and my production skills are no longer needed, I'll be set for a career as the new Fabio."

Heidi rolled her eyes. Her intervention years ago had saved the destruction of Quentin's self-esteem. Dressed in flea-market fashion and hair appropriate for London's underground, Heidi had possessed a sense of self rare in one so young.

Knowing what she wanted had never been a problem. It was the acquisition that had given her grief. Quentin had seen her blow off convention and chase her dream her way. He'd trusted her direction.

And it seemed she'd created a monster. Or a monster stud, she amended as the thoroughbred leaned past her shoulder to check his reflection in the mirror behind the bar.

She watched the pretentious male ritual with great amusement. But she had to admit he was gorgeous, what with the combination of his golden hair and stylish need to shave. The head-to-toe black in silk and linen and leather was the perfect canvas for his sun god coloring.

"Get a lot of mileage out of that hair, do you?" she asked.

It took five seconds for Quentin's gaze to skim her lap. "More mileage than you get out of that dress."

Dang it. Heidi crinkled her nose and adjusted one sliding shoulder strap. "This seemed like a good idea at the time."

Taking in the whole of her outfit, Quentin glanced at his watch. "It seems like a good idea now, too."

When had flirting ever been so easy, so fun? So perfectly, harmlessly nonthreatening all the way around? She'd missed Quentin's quick wit. She should've stayed in touch. Should've considered what she would be leaving behind when she ran.

Meeting his gaze, she lifted her chin and her beer. "You wouldn't be coming on to me, would you?"

Quentin gave her another head-to-toe once-over, forced up one roguish eyebrow. "I think that could be arranged."

Heidi smacked his shoulder. "If I didn't know you better, I'd think you were serious."

He looked down at her, his blue eyes narrowed, thoughtful. Devilish. His smiling mouth equally fiendish. "If I didn't know you better, I would be serious."

She'd walked right into that one. "First you cast aspersions on my roots...uh, the roots of my hair. Now you're disparaging my feminine allure. I see a lawsuit in your future, buster."

He made a face of insulted feelings and boosted up onto the now vacant stool next to hers. "Me? Disparage the Mighty Heidi Malone?"

Her bottle came down with a thud on the bar. Just like old times, the battle of wits and words was on, as if fifteen minutes had passed instead of fifteen years. This time, however, she had a better arsenal. And a bigger vocabulary.

Her smile was well sugared. Mighty Heidi Malone had intimidated worse characters than this one on her climb from the bottom of her life to the top. "You're lucky you got your dig in while the night is still young and I'm still forgiving. Because the next person to make reference to that particularly loathsome nickname will feel the truth and the pain of how I earned it."

"I'll be sure and warn Ben," Quentin said too casually to be casual.

Dang it. The air and the bluster whooshed from Heidi's sails. Again she tugged down her skirt, pulled up her shoulder strap, and put on her cool indifference to the subject of Ben Tannen. "Ben? He's here?"

"I haven't seen him." Quentin glanced around the crowded bar. Stopped. Rubbed the bristly growth on his chin. Then his gaze slid back to Heidi's. Slowly he nodded, as if a lightbulb had dropped from the sky and shattered on impact with his thick male skull. "That's why you came, isn't it? For Ben."

"What? Of course not," she lied. "I came to see old friends. You. And Jack and Randy." Her eye caught the mirrored image of the room as she made her point. Neither man appeared in her reflected field of vision. Yet a growing awareness of stares directed her way slid along her exposed skin like the cold sweat on the longneck in her hand.

She shook off the weirdness and turned to face her friend. "I've looked for both of them. But so far I've only been able to place a couple of people." It felt strange admitting she'd had no close friends beyond Quentin and Jack and Randy and...Ben, until she realized she had even fewer close friendships now. There was Georgia. And then there was...well, Georgia.

Funny that success and solitude were married in her mind, she thought, sipping the last of the one beer she'd allow herself tonight. Having lost touch with

Quentin made her realize what a double-sided coin she'd chosen to flip when professional success became the driving force in her life.

She sighed. "I guess I should've been more involved in high school, you know? But I spent so much time and energy making plans to get out that making friends didn't seem a priority." When Quentin didn't immediately respond, she glanced up into a face that must've broken a dozen female hearts by now. "What?"

"I think I'm offended. Or insulted. Or both." His considering look certainly hinted at the one or the other. He decided. And nodded. "Yep. Definitely both."

She frowned, not yet sure if he was serious. "Why do you say that? What I said about friends not being a priority? C'mon. That just came off the top of my head. You know I didn't mean you."

The break of pool balls clattered in the background. "That's good to hear."

Heidi turned her stool in order to face him directly. "Quentin, I would've dropped out our freshman year if it hadn't been for your friendship."

"You weren't old enough to drop out." He scolded her, flicking the end of her nose with his finger. Classic avoidance and change of subject.

"And you think age would've stopped me?" She wrapped her fingers around his wrist. Her touch and her tone both demanded he listen. "You were what stopped me, you goof. You wouldn't let me quit."

"Hell, no, I wouldn't let you quit. No one else was as honest with me as you were."

"Ah, yes." Heidi smiled at the memories singing close to the surface. "About your songs?"

Quentin grimaced and agreed. "They weren't songs. They were crap. You knew that. I knew that. But everyone else, my family, Randy, even Jack...no one else wanted to be honest. They wanted my crap to succeed."

She'd been so in awe of his musical intuition then. And so proud of him now. "I knew what you did well. And you are why we won so many awards in band. You know how to put the songs together. Which I understand has earned you an award or two to hang on your wall."

"Statuettes don't hang well on walls," he replied then raised a hand to order a drink of his own.

"Arrogant beast."

Amused, Quentin lifted his strong chin and looked down at Heidi. "I believe the industry rags are currently calling me Marks the Shark. I'm a firm believer in my own press."

She rolled her eyes. "And how much did you have to pay for that one?"

Leaning both elbows behind him on the bar, he inclined his head toward the crowded room. "Not as much as I'd pay for the type of attention you're getting."

"I was wondering about that. The looks, that is. Not your ridiculous appraisal of my diversionary worth." Her chuckle was not convincingly delivered. But what she felt wasn't funny. She wasn't sure if she was uncomfortable. Or just out of time and place. "They're staring at me like they don't know who I am."

"Think again, girl." Quentin shook his head. "They're staring because they didn't know you had legs. Or shoulders. Or—"

"Stop right there. Of course I had legs, uh, have legs. And shoulders. And—" she waved a hand "—other things."

"Like hair?"

"Yes. Like hair. Which I'm sure has a lot to do with it. I wouldn't expect anyone to recognize me now when I was invisible then." She affected a shudder. "I was such a joke."

Quentin laughed. "You never knew, did you?"

"Knew what?"

Mischief and devilment and charm turned up high, he reached for the flyaway strand of her hair again and let it slide through his fingers. "What I wouldn't pay to be a fly on your shoulder this weekend."

She had no clue what he was talking about and wasn't even sure she wanted to know. "Arrogant beastly tease."

Quentin laughed. "So fill me in. Tell me what the years have made of Mighty Heidi and I'll tell you about Marks the Shark."

"You've got a deal. On one condition." She glanced at the closest pool table.

Quentin followed her gaze. Looked back. Arched one Brad Pitt brow. "You're not serious."

"Of course I'm serious. Why wouldn't I be?" She was all innocence when called for.

And Quentin was all guilt. "You don't remember what happened last time we played pool?"

"Of course I remember." It had been September of their junior year. The night had grown long. Tempers short. And teenage hormones ran high. She wasn't likely to forget the night that had been the beginning of the end of a very long nine academic months.

She slipped from the bar stool, adjusted her dress from here to Sunday and hooked her arm through Quentin's. "Then let's go before Ben shows up to spoil my fun."

"Your idea of fun is what I'm afraid of," Quentin said. "I don't think my heart can take a repeat."

Heidi led the way, casting Quentin the smile of a vamp. "Don't worry. Since we played that last time? I haven't once stopped a game to take off my clothes."

Junior year

"I'M NOT GETTING OUT of the car." Heidi crossed her arms, drew up her knees and pouted. Coming here...here, of all places. Uh-uh. No way. Not after the day she'd had.

Quentin draped a wrist over the Bug's steering wheel and glared across the dark interior of the car. "You know, Heidi, you can be such a stupid dork at times."

Ha. That's what he thought. If anyone was stupid it was that slut, Maryann Stafford. No. If anyone was stupid it was Ben. Come to think of it, he was a slut, too.

Heidi pushed her chin and her lip out farther. "I didn't know we were coming here to practice. I thought we were meeting at the band hall."

"What's wrong with you? We practice at Ben's house all the time. Jeez." Quentin wrenched open his door, climbed out and slammed it hard enough to jar Heidi from her mope.

So what if they practiced at Ben's house all the time? It didn't mean they had to tonight. And she wasn't going to. Not after spending the entire hour of gym class today listening to Maryann Stafford run her mouth about what happened when she lost the top of her two-piece in Ben's pool this summer.

The passenger side door groaned as Quentin pulled it open. Heidi shoved her way out of the car, but left her horn in the back seat.

"Will you get your butt in gear?" Quentin yelled. He took hold of her empty hand, realized it was empty, grumbled under his breath as he reached back into the car. Horn and Heidi in tow, he trudged up the long pebbled walk to the Tannens' front door. "You're being a real jerk, you know that?"

"You call me one more name and you're history, Queenie Boy." Adding a tantrum to her sulk, Heidi fought Quentin's hold, pulling free as the door to the Tannen mansion opened. Quickly, she straightened her vest and T-shirt, but it wasn't Ben who greeted them.

"Quentin. Heidi." Ben's father—The Royal Tannen, as Heidi called him—acknowledged them both with a nod. He stood in the arched threshold surrounded by dark wood and white tile and light fixtures brighter than the bulbs glowing from inside. With a newspaper folded beneath one elbow, a drink gripped in one hand, he gestured toward the rear wing of the house. "The boys are up in the game room. Waiting."

"Thank you, sir." Quentin started forward, his

glare daring Heidi not to follow. She'd follow all right...

"It's my fault we're late," she said airily, as The Royal Tannen shut the heavy door. She gestured with one careless hand. Too bad she didn't have a mouthful of bubble gum to pop for the full brainless effect.

"See, my mom got fired today and was crying into the last beer of a six-pack when I got home from school. I couldn't leave her like that, ya know? So Quentin helped me get her to bed. Once she was asleep, we hurried right over."

"I see," Ben's father said, though from the granite set of his features, Heidi was surprised he was able to squeeze out a word. "Well—" he cleared his throat "—I hope things...she...is feeling better tomorrow."

"Thank you, sir. I'll be sure and give her your best." Heidi trotted after Quentin who'd made a hasty escape down the long hallway. Her footsteps made no sound on the plush carpet. She caught up with him at the staircase that wound to the game room above the three-car garage. "You could've waited."

He whirled on her at the third step. "What's wrong with you? You got PMS or something?"

She trudged past him, stomping her way up the circular ascent. What was wrong with her? Besides the ugly picture of Ben and Maryann that wouldn't go away? For one thing, she had an unemployed drunk for her only parent.

Her mother's latest episode meant little chance of affording anything but community college—if even that—next fall. But even worse, it meant she wouldn't be leaving home any time soon. That she'd be stuck with the alcohol, the anger, the affairs and the attic for who knew how much longer.

"I do *not* have PMS." She stopped at the top of the stairs and snarled down at Quentin. "What I have is a serious loathing for Ben Tannen...may he and all his money drown in his stupid swimming pool," she finished under her breath.

Quentin reached her then and stood toe to toe, nearly nose to nose, certainly eye to eye. "What you have is a serious attitude problem. Get rid of it. Now. I'm not going to have my chance for a first place ensemble win next weekend blown away by whatever's eating at you."

They stood fuming at one another there in a circle of yellow light. The paneled walls of the landing were dark, the ceiling high. The dangling chandelier gaudy and pretentious. Heidi wanted to puke. A chandelier. In a hallway. Her bedroom wasn't even this big.

She was the first to look away because she knew she was being unfair. Her reactions to anything involving Ben, even the most bubble-brained gossip, had been two years in the making. Today just proved that she had a big problem on her hands. One she'd been avoiding. One due to come to a head by the end of this year. Certainly by the end of next. Their last year.

That was the biggest part of what was wrong with her. Dealing with overwhelming feelings that she didn't want and would go nowhere because she and Ben were about as compatible as a gallon of gas and a Bic lighter. "Look, Quentin. You don't understand."

"Then tell me," he pleaded, his voice low, insistent. "C'mon. That's what friends are for."

But she couldn't for that very reason. Because as frustrated as she was over her home life and college funding and the top to Maryann Stafford's two-piece, she didn't want to bother Quentin with her problems. Not when he was staring a blue-ribbon weekend in the face. He needed this win to prove to himself that he had the musical talent to live his dream.

Dreams meant a lot. Or so she'd heard.

"Look," she began again, only to be cut short by a long rectangle of light thrown from the game room door. She looked up; Ben's silhouette—tall and broad-shouldered, that of a man—filled the frame as if backlit by a bright sun.

Tension rolled from him in waves, in the rigid way he held his head, in the firm fixed grip he had on the door facing, in the no-nonsense way he stood there and waited wearing a designer logo T-shirt and stylishly ripped jeans.

He'd never had Heidi's problem of control. She tended to bite her tongue way after the fact. Which made it easy for her to recognize that very struggle within him now.

"Where the hell have y'all been?" he asked in that too-deep voice that had Heidi closing her eyes for strength. Why did he have to be so...so...dang it, she couldn't even narrow what she thought about him down to one word.

"Hang on to your shorts, Ace," she yelled back, not bothering to spare Ben a direct eye-contact glance. Looking up, she gave Quentin a half smile, a lift of one shoulder and then she said, "I'm fine. And I'm sorry. Let's go practice."

They did, for two hours without a break. To Heidi

every second, every minute dragged. She wanted not to be here tonight more than any of the other times in her life when she'd wished she were someplace else.

She had to be crazy to be so torn up inside. It wasn't like she expected Ben to be a virgin. But Maryann Stafford? Heidi grimaced, missed a note, caught Quentin's glare and shrugged an apology.

And it wasn't like law school was forever out of her reach. But her future plans to educate women about their rights, to keep others such as her mother from becoming victims of the system, to ensure they received the benefits they deserved, had been moved another few years down the road.

She tried so hard to let the music take her away. But every time she felt she'd conquered the emotional bombs of the day, a fierce pounding detonated behind her eyes, fired against her temples, exploded inside her skull.

The headache couldn't be blamed on her internal battle. The source was clearly external: Ben was mad and his drums were loud. Instinctively, she knew the reason. He'd heard second- or third- or fourth-hand gossip of Maryann Stafford's tales.

Heidi couldn't stand the tension a minute more. She opened her eyes and glanced his way; his gaze was fixed on her. He followed every move, his mouth set hard, his eyes flinty, sweat-drenched locks of his hair whipping about his face as he ripped into the rhythm of the song.

This wasn't like Ben. To be this wild, his attention focused elsewhere while instinct drove the beat. She knew him well enough not to be frightened of whatever he had on his mind, but she was uneasy. Uneasy enough to call it quits. She set down her sax midnote. The rest of the song fizzled one player at a time. The drums were the last to cease.

Crossing the room, she leaned a hip on the corner of the pool, er, *billiard* table. She'd found a distraction. "Let's play a game."

Randy and Jack were quick to follow; Quentin and Ben reluctantly gave in. There were times she got her way because she was *the girl*. As a rule, she didn't take that advantage. Tonight was an exception.

Heidi pulled the balls from the billiard pockets and settled them into the rack, rolling each until its position suited her mood. "Since it's my game, I'll rack 'em. Ben can break. He seems to be in a destructive mood tonight."

Ben grabbed a cue from the custom-built rack. He pushed back the wet strands of hair that hung long past his brow. His eyes were green and glittered like shards of splintered anger. "At least I'm not *self*-destructive."

Heidi bristled. Behind her, Quentin cleared his throat. The friendly warning lifted her hackles higher. "But just think. If you were, your daddy could pay to have you fixed." She lifted the rack, stepped back and waited.

Randy guffawed and Jack snickered from where they'd perched expectantly on the cushions of the white leather game room sofa. Ben's icy glare had Randy studying the gold-and-brown patterned carpet between his spread feet, Jack slumping back to fiddle with the controls on the stereo system until Duran Duran rocked the room.

Ben's break was clean and hard, but then practice

gave perfect boys flawless skill. He'd had years of tutoring, pampering, silver-spoon feeding. Why shouldn't his break be as faultless as the crystal prisms of the chandelier lighting the landing?

Shot after expert shot stoked Heidi's temper. Irrational temper, her rational side knew. But Ben Tannen had everything. Everything, dang it. And one piece at a time, with the exact precision with which cue tip met cue ball, her future was dying before her eyes.

She watched his stance, his concentration, the culmination of seventeen years of instruction in what society deemed proper, handed down from The Royal Tannen on high. Ben's way in the world had been bought and paid for with Tannen money. And all he'd had to earn was his father's respect, which he had.

He was a perfect father's perfect son. But she hated him the most because he gave her no real reason to hate him at all. He must have sensed the burning in her chest. He finally looked up into her eyes...and missed the shot.

She blinked hard against overwhelming emotions, against the feelings so close to the surface she felt as if her skin would burst. Right now, she wanted perfect Ben to feel as miserable as she did. "Whew. I was beginning to wonder if I was going to have to go home without taking a shot at your balls, Ben."

"Jeez, Heidi." Quentin began to pace.

She laughed, feeling strangely as if she were careening out of control. Shrugging out of her long crocheted vest, she took her position, called her first shot and expertly sent the ball zooming into the pocket. The next sailed perfectly. As did the one following.

She sized up the table, visualized her next shot and made the biggest mistake of her life by taking her eyes off the ball. From beneath her lashes, she looked across the table at Ben who wasn't following the strategy of her game at all, but was staring at the thin white T-shirt stretched over her chest. He had fire in his eyes.

The volcano erupted. Lava spewed, an inferno boiling up from the hell of a day she'd had. With a loud, "Arghhh," she slammed the cue to the felt, reached for her hem and jerked the T-shirt over her head.

"There! Is that better?" Two of the boys behind whooped and hollered; the third yelled a pained, "Shut the hell up!" The one facing her directly refused to look away from her eyes. She'd fix that.

"Wait." She went on, whipping off her bra before she changed her mind. "I wouldn't want you to strain your eyes or your imagination wondering how I compare to Maryann Stafford."

Ben's chest rose and fell in near-breathless pants. His eyes were wild and bright when he looked over her head toward Quentin and the other two boys. A brow went up. He nodded. Heidi waited for an eternity for Ben to say something, anything.

When he did, he didn't even speak to her but to the boys behind. "I'll take Heidi home. Quentin'll give y'all a ride."

"C'mon, Ben—"

"Practice is over." He didn't even let Randy finish his complaint. Ben's commanding tone was surprisingly calm. He rounded the end of the table, snagged Heidi's T-shirt from the floor and held it out to her with a hand that trembled as he spoke to the others. "Leave the instruments. I'll bring them to band tomorrow."

Heidi grabbed the T-shirt and held it to her chest. Behind her she heard lowing moans and the shuffle of six overgrown feet on indoor/outdoor carpeting. The longer it took Quentin to herd his reluctant cattle, the faster her rush of brazenness trickled away. God, she was going to vomit.

The game room door closed and the three of them were finally alone. She and Ben and her behavior. She'd taken off her shirt—still had it off, in fact—and he hadn't even looked. She couldn't decide whether to be humiliated or insulted or to sink to the floor behind the table and hide.

What she finally did was slip her shirt over her head and down, tugging the hem as low as it would go. Her vest was at her feet, her bra on the floor closer to Ben's. Definitely closing in on humiliation, she managed to retrieve both pieces of clothing, shrug into the vest and stuff the bra into the pocket of her jeans without once looking at his face.

She'd started disassembling her sax when he spoke.

"Heidi, Maryann's lying."

Her nod acknowledged that she'd heard him, not that she believed him. She wasn't in the mood to believe him. All she wanted to do was start this day over from the blast of her alarm clock this morning.

"She didn't lose her top in the pool." He shuffled from one foot to the other. "Well, she lost it, but it wasn't like it was an accident or anything. You know Maryann."

"Not as well as you do, apparently." She locked the saxophone case and turned; she locked her jaw as well. It kept her chin from quivering. "You can take me home now."

Ben pushed back the hair from his forehead. "Dammit, Heidi. Nothing really happened."

"Really?" The burn in her stomach flared. "What does that mean, 'Nothing *really* happened.'? That nothing happened at all? That whatever happened didn't mean anything?" Her voice and temper rose in unison. "That everything's okay because we *all* know Maryann?"

"What do you want me to say?" he asked, standing with his arms crossed, the pool table squarely between them.

His defensiveness answered her question. She grabbed her sax and lifted her chin. "I don't want you to say anything. I want you to take me home."

"I'm not taking you home until you listen to me." He started forward.

She headed toward the door. "Fine. I'll walk."

He changed directions, rounding the table to head her off. "You can't walk."

"I have two legs. I most certainly can."

"That's not what I meant. It's too far." He'd reached the door now and blocked it with his body. "And it's not exactly the safest neighborhood to be walking through at night."

His lack of tact and consideration amazed her at times. She wondered if he'd taken lessons in *holier-*

than-thou along with deportment. "I live in that neighborhood, Ben."

"Cripes, Heidi. Do you have to twist everything I say?" Broad hands gripped her shoulders, green eyes made a great show of caring. "I don't want anything to happen to you."

"Thanks for the concern. But I'd rather take care of myself. I can make sure nothing happens to me." She shrugged off his hold, took a step back while he crossed his arms and leaned back on the door. "You see, I'm not Maryann Stafford."

"You're still not walking home."

She shook her head. He was totally impossibly arrogant at times, but she didn't hate him anymore. Never *had* hated him, in fact. What she felt deserved a deep and thorough and very private exploration, but not tonight. Not tonight. "I know you're used to getting your way, but it's not going to happen this time. Now, move please, so I can go."

He sidestepped, but left his hand on the doorknob. "If you don't want me to drive you, I'll ask my dad to take you."

"Uh, no thanks."

"Then I'll call you a cab."

Hysterical laughter bubbled up. She pressed shaky fingers to her forehead and sighed. "You and your money."

"What about my money?" he asked but he did finally open the door.

She didn't want to talk or explain or answer another single question. She was tired and she wanted to go home. That was all. "You know how it is. The rich get richer, the poor pay taxes." Then she tried to bite her tongue, but the words had already rolled from the end. "And if there's anything left they might be able to afford tuition."

"What are you talking about?"

"Nothing, Ben. Just take me home." Head held high, she left the game room. Ben followed, slamming the door so hard the walls rattled.

His steps were heavy and close behind her, but she didn't move aside. And she swore no matter how much money she made in her lifetime, she would never hang a chandelier in a hallway.

"Eight ball in the corner pocket." Heidi made the call, made the shot and made the crowd of onlookers cheer as she whipped the pants off Quentin Marks. Figuratively speaking, of course.

As she'd told him earlier, clothes had not been removed during a game she'd played now for fifteen years. "Best two out of three? Winner buys dinner? I'm dying for a burger and fries."

"You want a burger, you got it. But the competition's over for tonight. Gotta save my strength for tomorrow's softball tourney." He took her cue, laid it across the table next to his and wrapped her in a bear hug that crushed a rush of laughter from her chest. "Damn but it's good to see you, Heidi."

"I'll second that."

Oh...nooo. That voice. Not that voice. She whispered up to Quentin because whispering was all she could coax from her voice box. "Tell me that was all in my imagination. Tell me I'm hearing things."

"You are hearing things." Quentin glanced over his shoulder, then, smiling, looked back and down into Heidi's face. "You're hearing exactly what you thought you heard."

Slowly, Heidi extricated herself from Quentin's arms. Her hands remained on his chest. She needed that moment of stabilizing support before she stepped out from behind the shield of his larger broader body and faced the owner of that voice.

Ben Tannen.

2

QUENTIN TURNED AROUND, his body momentarily shielding Heidi's as he held out his hand to shake Ben's. "Hey, Ben. Lookin' good for a small-town newspaperman...except for that gray, there. Age taking up where stress left off?"

Newspaperman? Small town? What was wrong with this picture? What had happened to the big city, the big daily, the big editorial position?

And what had happened to Quentin's priorities? Heidi didn't care about the past fifteen years of Ben's life but that was no reason for Quentin not to tell her every detail.

"At least I don't look like a Samson wannabe," Ben said, his voice an even deeper version, if that was possible, of the one Heidi remembered.

She didn't really want to remember how that voice had made her face flush and her heart trip. She didn't want to remember how beckoning was the safe harbor of that voice in the turbulent waters that had been her life.

She leaned her forehead into the center of Quentin's back and anchored her fidgety hands at his waist. Next time she'd listen to Georgia—as much as it went against her personal karma to do so—and spend future weekends off in a more productive activity.

Like doing her nails.

Ben went on. "What happens if you cut off that tail, Marks? You lose your musical talent?"

Quentin chuckled, his shoulders shook. "If I find a Delilah worth cutting it for, you'll be the first to know. In fact, I'll give you and that weekly rag of yours the exclusive."

"Delilah, huh?" Ben did a quick clearing of his throat. "Wouldn't happen to be her nails there clawing into your shirt?"

Heidi made two fists even as Quentin took hold of both her hands and pried open her fingers. "Nope. I think this particular Delilah has another man's downfall on her dance card."

"Ha!" Heidi yelped and butted her forehead into Judas's back. Then she jerked her hands away and peered around Quentin's shoulder at the man she'd come here to forget.

How could she ever forget? Why, oh why had she thought time would make a difference? Her face burned, her belly trembled, her palms began to sweat. Her earlier schoolgirl jitters had been easily banished.

But that was before she'd laid eyes on Ben.

Jitters were nothing compared to the purely adult, purely female recognition of the temptation he offered, a temptation born of all things male—confidence, control, an acceptable measure of arrogance. He was a man secure in who he was and he was more, oh much more, than Heidi had expected to find.

He stood with a longneck dangling from the fingers of one hand, the other stuffed in the pocket of navy slacks with a custom-tailored fit. His hair was a richer, thicker brown than that of years ago and Quentin hadn't been kidding about the sprinkling of gray. The cut was definitely better than the rock 'n roll look he'd favored as a teen.

She'd never paid a lot of attention to the clothes Ben wore. At least compared to the attention she was paying now. Above the dark blue slacks, he wore a yellow crew-neck sweater of what appeared to be cashmere, the long sleeves bunched at his elbows. The pastel set off the dark shadow of his evening beard and his even darker hair.

The entire look was so fashionably casual that it screamed class and money. No, Heidi mentally corrected. What it screamed was Tannen. But for some reason that didn't turn her off the way it had in the past. In fact, she found herself quite turned on.

"Hello, Ben." *Long time no try to kill.* "It's been a while." *At least fifteen years and fifteen stitches.*

Ben frowned, and to Heidi's consternation, took his time taking in her short short skirt, her long long legs, her curled and colored hair. A sip from his longneck and still he took his time. So Heidi gave him plenty to look at.

Standing at enough of an angle that Ben wouldn't see more than she wanted him to see, she leaned down to adjust the strap of her strappy low-heeled sandal. Her nails were a seductively flirty red which helped with her seductively flirty move.

Her dress lifted in the back, lowered in the front, but all in a most tasteful display. Along with the rest of her education, Heidi had learned the difference between a thoughtful, artful exhibition and one fueled by emotion and made on the spur of the moment.

And the confidently controlled, arrogant man stood silent.

Ignoring Quentin's low chuckle and the impulse to jab an elbow into his midsection, Heidi straightened, slid her fingers into her hair and pushed it back from her face. Then she took a good look at Ben's eyes.

Her fingers slowed and slipped free. Her hair tumbled back into place and she lowered her arm. Her hand slid along her side to her hip, the move all the more enticing for its lack of guile. She knew that by the flare in Ben's eyes, a smoky reaction her outlandish display hadn't come close to producing.

He might stand there looking like a study in Tannen class and fashion, but Ben wasn't as coldly unaffected on the inside as his outward demeanor might indicate to those who didn't have Heidi's eye-to-eye perspective.

She wasn't sure what to do with the implications of that realization. Or what to do next. Even after he smiled and said, "Hello, Heidi," in that low sexy voice and she answered, "Hi," with as much calm as she could manage, she didn't know what to do next. So they stood there, both of them waiting, like the past would take care of itself if they gave it enough time.

"Tell you what," Quentin said, jumping ship when the silence grew to titanic proportions. "I'm going to let you two stand here and look at each other while I make the rounds. See if Jack or Randy decided to show their faces."

"Traitor," Heidi mumbled under her breath, shrugging off the hand Quentin had placed on her shoulder just as another couple walked up.

"I'm showing a lot more than my face, Queenie Boy. Just not enough to get arrested for."

"Randy!" Heidi took in the third of the four best friends she'd had in school.

His khaki slacks and crisp blue chambray shirt were as trendy as the clothes worn by both Ben and Quentin, as was the cut of his dark-brown hair. He was shorter than the other men, and stockier, and the looks that had been average in school had matured into a face that had Heidi catching a breath.

"Randy, you look great," she said and meant every word.

He gave her a loud smooch on the cheek and pulled back. "Nothing like the high-school jock with the big head and big mouth, eh?"

Quentin rubbed at the fuzz on his chin and considered Randy from all angles. "Big mouth? Big head? Yep, I'd say that's exactly what you look like."

"And you weren't a jock. You played golf," Ben added.

"Hey, hey, hey. I coulda played football. I *coulda* been a *contenda.* I coulda been king of the world instead of The King of The Deck." Randy raised his hands, wiggled his fingers. "But I had to save these jewels for my horn."

The group laughed as Quentin said, "Better a trophy case of blue ribbons than a perennial case of benchwarmer butt."

Offering Randy's female friend a silent apology for the exclusion, Heidi's hands went to her hips, her gaze from Randy to Quentin to Ben. "You guys! I swear y'all sound like you're still in high school."

"I thought that was the point of a *re*union." Ben gestured with his longneck. "*Re*membering."

"*Re*miniscing," Quentin said.

"*Re*gurgitating," Randy added.

Heidi groaned. "Well, at least give Randy a chance to introduce his date, not that she wants to meet any of you after all of that."

Randy placed his hand in the small of the woman's back. "Julie, this quick and witty bunch makes up three fifths of The Deck. Heidi Malone, Quentin Marks and Ben Tannen. And this is Julie Damon."

"Hi, Julie," Heidi began, warmly shaking hands with the petite, dark-haired woman. "I'm not sure what Randy's told you, but playing with this deck requires checking your sensitivity—not to mention your good taste—at the door." She punctuated her statement with a sharp glance at each of the three men.

"Speaking of bad taste, where is Jack?" Randy hooked a friendly elbow around Julie's neck.

Patting his hand where it rested on her shoulder, Julie smiled at Heidi with shared female long-suffering. "I've known Randy awhile now. I'm on my second fitting of asbestos skin so don't worry about me. *Re*visit your memories to your heart's content."

"Well, well, well." Quentin rubbed his hands together, the devil all in black. "I do believe Julie will fit right in as The Deck *re*verts to a weekend of immaturity."

"Be warned." Julie pointed a finger in Quentin's direction. "I *re*fuse to wear a playing-card sandwich board."

He shook his head vigorously. "No need to advertise what's an obvious ten."

"A ten dressed to the nines," Randy added, wiggling both brows as he took in Julie's red silk oriental-style pantsuit.

A collective groan rose from the group. Julie put up a hand. "Enough already! Randy, buy me a beer. If you're going to work your way through the entire deck, I'm going to need *re*inforcement."

"Yes, dear. Anything you say, dear." Randy signaled a passing waitress and ordered drinks for the group. The conversation deteriorated into numeric clichés until Randy managed a segue from card decks to the upper deck of the Houston Astros' new baseball stadium and the home-run distances involved.

The talk turned to baseball then and Heidi's gaze moved over the small circle of men, her expression softening with memories. She studied the obvious changes in hairlines and muscle definition, the outcome of games played by the years and Mother Nature.

She studied the subtler changes as well. There was Quentin's sense of confidence and self, which she knew stemmed from the success he'd found in his music, a success all the more priceless for being his heart's calling.

Not many people were able to make that claim. She felt a tightening in her chest, realizing what a lucky man was her friend, and how lucky she was to call him one. She made a vow right then to get his number and remember to call him more often than once in half a lifetime.

Randy also appeared to have done well for himself, but then she'd never expected less. He may not have had Ben's wealth or Quentin's talent, but he'd come from a solid family, had kept a near-4.0 grade point average throughout school.

He hadn't shared that secret with many. It wasn't cool to be smart. He'd had the brains but not the maturity to use his intelligence to his advantage, and the one time Heidi had tried to do it for him...well, that was one memory she'd sooner forget.

And then there was Ben. Oh, Ben. Heidi released a shuddering sigh. He'd been as hard on her as she'd been on Randy. As responsible as Quentin was for keeping her from dropping out, Ben had been the reason she'd stayed.

From that first time she'd walked into that freshman band hall and seen the boy who had everything, she'd known that there would be a day when she and Ben—

"I can't believe these guys," Julie said, her laughter cutting into Heidi's musing. "It's like they see each other every day. Men seem to be able to pick up where they left off, down to the very conversation they dropped fifteen years ago."

The men's conversation was working its way from professional sports to locker-room tales. Heidi rolled her eyes. "I think that's because men have the same conversation for years. They just switch the references. From VHS to DVD. From Reagan to Clinton. From Farrah Fawcett to Pamela Lee."

Julie laughed. "I think you're right. We, on the

other hand, have progressed from fashion and relationships to fashion, relationships and the stock market."

"Much more progressive," Heidi agreed, giving up
all semblance of a straight face and glancing around
the room. Video games sound effects and the flashing
colors of pinball lights were the trademarks of the
young and carefree.

It was a night made for fun and laughter and she
planned to relax and enjoy. "Do you and Randy work
for the same brokerage house?"

"Actually, he works for my firm's biggest compet-
itor, damn those no-compete clauses." Julie gestured
with her drink toward the man in question. Her face
softened as she talked. "We tend to unwind on the
same nights at the same club. When the market's up
we celebrate. When it's down, well, those are the latest nights depending on how much of whose money
we've lost."

Following the direction of Julie's gaze, Heidi
glanced at the men who had settled into a deeper conversation. Ben had his back to her, giving her a
chance to admire and appreciate what the years had
wrought...but only briefly because Quentin caught
her wandering eye and winked. She glared back, re-
sisted sticking out her tongue, then looked at Randy.

"It's hard to think of Randy as stressed, even as intense as he was in school," she said, her gaze returning to Julie. When the other woman frowned, Heidi
explained. "It's just that his intensity was so focused
on fun that it didn't come across as a negative tension."

"Trust me. He's a real type A personality. I recog-

nize the signs all too well because I'm just like him."
Julie leaned her head to the side. The ends of her dark
hair brushed against the red silk and her mouth
twisted wryly.

It was a look and expression of body language that
put Heidi's female intuition on high alert. "That must
make for an interesting relationship."

"We don't really have a relationship," Julie hurried
to say. "We're just friends. He thinks of me as one of
the guys."

Heidi laughed. "Now that sounds familiar."

"How so?"

She nodded toward the male members of The
Deck. "That's exactly how this bunch thought of me
in school. Just one of the guys."

"You're kidding, right?" Julie's wide-eyed expression authenticated her skepticism. "You thought you
were one of the guys?"

"I didn't think so." She inclined her head. "They
did. It was an all-for-one, one-for-all kinda thing."

This time it was Julie with the discerning nod and
judiciously narrowed eyes. "Then this should be
quite the interesting weekend."

"I don't understand. Oh, wait." The lightbulb
blinked on and Heidi saw past her confusion.
"Randy's been telling stories, hasn't he. Filling you in
on our escapades so you wouldn't feel left out this
weekend?"

Finished sipping her beer, Julie shook her head.
"Randy's been telling me about The Deck for years.
I've never met Ben or Quentin, but I knew both of
them the minute we walked up." One brow arched,
Julie added, "And I certainly knew you."

"That one was a given. I am the only female."

"No. It wasn't just the sex thing."

"Hmm. Then it was probably The Joker thing. You did catch me post-performance." Not exactly one of her finer moments this evening, either. "I never did think of myself as being particularly funny. Though I do remember a lot of, 'We're not laughing at you, we're laughing with you.'"

"From what I understand, laughing was only the half of it."

This was growing more cryptic by the moment. "Again. You've lost me. I'm sorry."

"Don't be," Julie said and put up one hand to wave off Heidi's apology. "I'm being too vague, I know. I was just curious to see if Randy was right. That you didn't know what everyone really thought. Or how they felt about you."

Heidi let out a sigh that was as much frustration as anything. "This isn't the first time I've heard that tonight. Quentin said something very similar."

"After witnessing the dynamics of this group? I'm taking Randy at his word." Julie leaned a little closer, turned her back to the men. "Trust me. Not a boy in The Deck thought of you as *one of the guys.*"

"Ah, methinks Randy's been telling more than tales." Heidi laughed, but her curiosity had been aroused. Surely she hadn't been *that* blind in high school? So blind that she'd've missed what Julie's comment seemed to imply? "It's just silly to think any of them thought of me as more than The Joker."

Julie's smile was have-it-your-way smug. "Maybe not. Still, Ben might not've reacted to that temptation you offered earlier, but Randy nearly swallowed his tongue. And Quentin's eyes weren't far from popping out of his head.''

Heidi wasn't sure which of Julie's observations was responsible for the wave that rolled through her stomach. Quentin's eyeballs, Randy's tongue or the fact that a complete stranger picked up on the subtle vibes Heidi had aimed Ben's way.

Okay. Not so subtle. Still, Julie must be psychic. "I'm sure you're exaggerating." Or better yet, imagining things. Heidi preferred the latter. It would make for an uncomfortable weekend if she couldn't relax with the few old friends she'd come to see. The stares from the classmates she didn't remember were quite enough to deal with, thank you very much.

Julie shook her head. "I'm not. And I'll prove it to you." She lowered her voice even further. "Now, while I'm talking to you, look over to where the three cards in question are deep in flashback."

Heidi looked that way briefly. "I see them. Now what?"

Julie's dark eyes took on the sheen of a woman with a mission. "Give it a full fifteen seconds, but keep your eyes on those three. I can guarantee each of them will catch you catching them unawares."

"And what do I do when I catch them?"

"Enjoy making them squirm, then throw them back. See, it won't be that you just catch their eyes. Trust me. It won't be your eyes they're looking at. Randy will blush. I don't know about the other two, but that's a given."

Sure enough, Randy blushed. And true to Julie's word he wasn't caught looking into Heidi's eyes. By the time their eyes did meet, he'd taken the full look she'd solicited unsuccessfully from Ben. She delivered a glare that said, "Shame on you," and his color deepened.

"Am I right?" Julie asked to keep to keep the faux conversation going.

"So far, yes. Randy looks good wearing red. But I'm going to give him the benefit of the doubt. You have to understand that I look nothing like I did in high school. I was punk in a school where the word meant troublemaker, not fashion statement."

Julie nodded, but didn't seem convinced. "Nothing from the other two?"

"Well," Heidi began, realizing that while Quentin's dramatic gestures punctuated whatever story he was telling, his gaze was a study in male appreciation. It wasn't lewd or even suggestive. It was the look of an artist taking pleasure in the end result wrought by years of creative effort. And it was disconcerting because Heidi had never thought of herself as a work of art.

She didn't like the idea that there was a part of herself she'd missed seeing. "Okay. I'll give you two out of three. But Ben won't bite." That she would stake her career on.

"Trust me. Ben will do a lot more than bite. He's got that look."

"That look?" Heidi had a hard time keeping her head from swinging around.

"Determination. Almost like you and he might have unfinished business?"

Dang it. Heidi could only stare, meeting the other woman's intuitively shrewd look. If Julie, a virtual stranger, was so perceptive, picking up on the connection Heidi had to Ben, what was going on in the minds of the people here who knew?

Oh, boy. Stupid, stupid, stupid. Heidi had really missed the boat. That's what all the stares were about. People weren't seeing a work of art or wondering who she was. They knew.

And they were on the edges of their seats, waiting for the impending Jerry Springer confrontation between the assaulter and the assaultee.

"Unfinished business?" Heidi laughed because it was more decorous than releasing the hysterical scream clawing at the back of her throat. "And when you're not buying and selling stocks you practice psychology?"

"I know. I'm terrible." Julie pressed a hand to her breast. "But I'm an inveterate people watcher. Besides, I know how Ben got that sexy scar across his jaw."

Heidi groaned. "Randy's tales again."

"Let's put it this way. When he told me about the reunion, I invited myself along as his date."

Great. Julie probably even knew about the game of strip pool. "Well, The Deck may not provide a weekend of entertainment value, but you should have a good time. After spending four years with these guys, it'll be nice to have a female friend to hang out with."

Julie glanced around the club. The neon bar lights caught the shine in her red silk. "I wouldn't think you'd need me for that with all the females here to choose from."

Heidi was rather embarrassed to admit how closed off she'd kept herself from the rest of her classmates. "I stayed pretty focused in school. Which meant a lot of studies and a lot of band practice. Plus, I was a bit of an outcast. I never did have a lot of friends."

"So, why'd you come?"

"To the reunion?"

Julie nodded and Heidi had to decide between complete and partial honesty. Had she come to see her few old friends? To finish what was never settled between herself and Ben?

To revisit the place from which she'd been so determined to escape that she'd been unable to hold on long enough and prove that she had nothing to be ashamed of, no reason to run?

Whoa! Where had that come from?

"Hey, I think the band's finally going to play," Randy said, walking up and cutting off further conversation.

Ben and Quentin followed, the men rejoining the women and saving Heidi from further bothersome self-examination—which was especially nice because Ben chose to stand at her shoulder and she could hardly concentrate when she felt the pinpoint pricks of prying eyes.

Jerry Springer, here we come!

She turned her attention to the stage where the five-member band was taking up instruments, tuning, running riffs, adjusting mike stands and the rest of the steps required of an equipment check. It was easier to feign interest in the band's doings than to think of something to say to Ben with hundreds of antennae tuned their direction.

Not that he appeared anxious in the least to talk to her. In fact, their mutual silence seemed to suit him just fine. He seemed to be biding his time, allowing the tension to build and settle heavily around Heidi's head and shoulders.

But the Mighty Heidi Malone wasn't about to so easily surrender her evening of fun or her peace of mind, whether to a real or an imagined intimidation. She shook off the cloak of impending doom and focused on the profile of the band's bass player instead.

He wore worn jeans over biker boots, a white T-shirt and dark shades. His hair, a nearly brown shade of blond, was wavy and brushed back from his face.

And just as the drummer counted out, "One, two, three, four," with the crack of drumstick on drumstick and the players burst into a cover of Bruce Springsteen's "Born In The USA," just as the entire club burst into loud applause and louder whoops and hollers, Heidi realized the bass player was none other than the missing member of The Deck. Jack Montgomery.

"That's Jack!" she yelled to no one in particular even though the music was too loud for anyone to hear.

Ben heard. He leaned forward, his chin at the lobe of her ear when he shouted, "His hobby. The band plays a lot of the small local clubs."

"They're great! What're they called?"

"Diamond Jack," Ben answered and laughed.

Heidi couldn't help but laugh in return. Jack was good. The band caught every nuance of the eighties hit and brought the song to life.

And Jack sang. Heidi had no idea that Jack sang. She backed up closer to Ben and said over her shoulder, "He's good. He's really good."

Ben nodded, leaned closer to be heard, his shoulder offering Heidi's a resting place. "He's good because he does it for fun. He says if he tried to make it a career, he'd crack."

"He told you all this?"

"Yeah. We've kept in touch since I moved back." After that, Ben fell silent, listening to the music and moving his body to the beat.

Heidi found herself compelled to do the same, found her movements in sync with Ben's, her hips brushing his thigh as she swayed. This contact was comfortable, the nonthreatening sort easily shared between friends of the opposite sex.

The accompanying tingle at the base of her spine was something else entirely. She'd ignore that, of course, because this was Ben and they had business to settle and scores of onlookers waiting.

For now she was determined to enjoy the music. And if touching Ben in this most casual way enhanced her enjoyment, well, she'd leave that cross-examination for later.

Diamond Jack had reached the end of the song. Jack had his hands overhead, clapping out the rhythm of the closing chorus and encouraging the crowd to do the same. He belted out the finale to roaring applause, then whipped off his sunglasses and threw them into the crowd.

"Welcome to 1984! The year of Big Brother!"

The party-goers shouted and cheered and clamored for more, then laughed even louder at the one loudly shouted "Boo!"

"C'mon, sport," Jack urged. "We'll get back to the nineties soon enough. For now, we're here to remind you of what exactly you looked like back in those good ol' days of parachute pants and acid-washed jeans!"

More cheers went up.

"Rattails and high hair!"

This time the response was moaning laughter.

"How about jams and jellies?" Jack looked out at the crowd from beneath a knowing brow. "And I'm not talkin' about food here."

Even Heidi giggled at that.

"Now, to get you in the mood for the rest of the weekend we have Springsteen and Styx, Journey and Genesis. And since there's no better way to get reacquainted than getting up close and personal, all you dudes grab you a valley girl and dance!"

The song began, Jack's voice making magic of a ballad as the crowd separated into couples. Ready to sit out the first of many dances, Heidi started toward the bar, only to find her way blocked by Ben.

3

SHE PLACED HER PALM IN HIS.

He wrapped his fingers over hers.

His touch was warm and her heart kicked out a beat. He raised one brow, nodded his head and then began to move.

His feet slipped between hers, left right, right left, his thigh pressed close. His strength was a comfort as only that of a man could be to a woman.

She relaxed against him, but didn't give herself up the way she could so easily have done. This was Ben, with whom she had no business getting intimate, no matter how intense the old feelings and the want she couldn't seem to shake.

Ben was the last mark she needed to wipe clean from the slate of her past. No, she hadn't been holding on to those years instead of getting on with her life. She'd moved forward with her life just fine.

But she couldn't put away the picture of who she'd once been until she dusted away this final cobweb.

So, why did her body pressed this close to his seem like a first step—a beginning instead of the ending, the healing, the catharsis it was supposed to be?

"You dance well." Ben's voice was pitched low, his words delivered to her ears alone. "I don't think we've ever danced together."

No. They'd been friends, but they'd run in different circles. And she'd have remembered feeling him, this way. She never had, and for a moment she closed her eyes and allowed herself to enjoy the sensation of being held in strong arms.

"Thank you. And you're right. We haven't. I don't think that we ever had an opportunity."

"Sure we had opportunity," he said, adjusting his hand on the small of her back until it felt like it belonged. "Homecoming. Valentine's Day. Prom."

Nothing like reality to whip off fantasy's cloak. Heidi pulled back to look into his eyes. She arched both brows in a silent waiting.

Ben frowned. "What?"

"Who am I, Ben?"

The frown disappeared. Amusement slid into place. "The Mighty Heidi Malone."

She growled, determined to deal with that later. "Okay, then. Who *was* I?"

He thought a minute as he moved to the music. "The Joker?"

"The Joker didn't dance."

"Hmm. You may be right," he said and they danced more, silently, privately, moving closer then apart as the music demanded.

This was so nice, this being held in Ben's arms. Too nice, in fact, for a moment that could be nothing but a moment.

The differences they had in the past weren't as apparent today, but they were still differences. Yes, Ben was the reason she was here. But she'd come to make amends, not for...this.

She hadn't expected him to feel so good standing

so close. She hadn't expected him to hold her, and to hold her so well. She'd thought she'd find a grown-up version of the boy she'd known.

But a boy didn't move this smoothly or hold a woman with this much confidence. A boy didn't anticipate a woman's moves, meet her needs, lead her exactly where she wanted to go.

The band switched to another ballad and when Ben silently asked for the next dance as well, Heidi answered his unspoken invitation with a nod.

"What brought you back to Sherwood Grove?" she asked, determined that this dance would be spent in conversation, not in reckless musings and physical appreciations leading nowhere.

Ben's chin nuzzled her ear then pulled back and spoke. "Stonebridge, actually. Not Sherwood Grove."

"Stonebridge. That's on the other side of Austin, right?" He nodded and she went on, rambling a bit because his mouth was so close and his lips, when he spoke, drew her attention, made her wonder—

Dang it. She was drifting again. "I think we drove through there once on the way to a band competition. If I remember, there was only one stoplight and a population sign bragging on the town's, what? Two thousand residents?"

"I think it was more than that. And it's up to about ten thousand now. Lots of folks scaling down, looking for a simpler life."

"Is that what you did?" It was hard to believe that of him. Of any Tannen.

He nodded again, shifted his hold on her hand. The music grew soft, Ben's touch that much softer, though his voice still carried a bit of an edge. "Pretty much. Took a while to get there."

"To Stonebridge? Or to needing Stonebridge?" The distinction was one Heidi knew well.

She'd left Sherwood Grove long after she'd reached the point of needing to leave. She just hadn't had the means to go—until it was offered. And offered by the boy this man had been.

Ben's chuckle rumbled deeply in his chest. The vibration met with no resistance as it settled behind Heidi's breastbone—way too close to her heart. She increased the distance between their bodies.

Ben stepped closer into her space. "I hadn't thought of it that way before, but you're right. I needed Stonebridge a long time before I arrived. It just took eight years, four career moves and one wife to get me there."

He'd been married. Or was still married. Damn that Quentin Marks and his nonmeddling, nongossip-mongering hide. Heidi corrected her second misstep and said, "How long have you been married?"

"Past tense." Ben's mouth lifted ruefully. "I wasn't sure if you knew that."

"No, but I'm not surprised. A Tannen is quite a catch. I would've been more surprised to find you'd stayed single." And now that she thought about it, this whole weekend would've been simpler if he *had* been married.

If Ben had been married, he wouldn't be holding her this close and she wouldn't be wanting him to and wondering why. She turned her wondering to his wife. "It wasn't Maryann Stafford, I hope."

Finally, Ben laughed. "No, she was a Katherine.

We met at University of Texas. Both journalism majors."

Katherine Tannen. Terrible-sounding name. "I'm sorry things didn't work out. Did you have children?" *Did she marry you for your money? Did she meet with your family's approval? Did you love her?*

"Me and Katherine?" Ben shook his head. "No. We both had careers that demanded twenty-four hours, seven days a week. That didn't leave a lot of time for talking about family much less doing anything about starting one."

He said the last with a sense of resignation more than a sense of regret. She tried to ignore the fact that he was talking about his married sex life, or lack thereof. No matter her flippant thoughts, she hated that he'd been unhappy.

"I suppose that's best. That you didn't have children. Since you didn't stay together, that is." Heidi grimaced. Did high school reunions automatically return one's social skills to those of an inept adolescent?

Ben used the hand holding hers to lift up her chin. His eyes glittered with a strangely suppressed energy. "Relax. We're just catching up on each other's lives. Ask whatever you want to ask."

Maybe if she thought of him as still married, she'd survive his touch and this dance. And maybe if she didn't wonder what he was holding in check, she'd survive the night. "Okay. I wasn't sure if I'd overstepped the bounds of reminiscing."

"Reminiscing is fine. Just spare me the regurgitating."

She laughed. "Randy, that rat. He hasn't changed.

And he's been telling a few too many tales to suit me."

"Tales? To Julie?" When Heidi nodded, Ben said, "They must've been good ones. You two seemed like the ones doing all the catching up."

"Just girl talk."

"Hmm. You didn't do much of that in school, did you?"

Heidi nearly stepped on his foot. "C'mon, Ben. It's been fifteen years, not fifty. You can't have forgotten that much by now. Who would I have made girl talk with in high school?"

"And now?"

Uh-oh. "Now what?"

"You have someone to make girl talk with now?"

"Of course I do." She had Georgia, so at least that wasn't a lie.

He pulled her tighter to his body. "What about boy talk?"

He held her close, his hold a taunt more than an embrace. Wariness stirred in her for the first time. "Boy talk?"

"Sure. You have anyone who whispers sweet nothings into your ear?" he asked, leaning forward to whisper into her ear.

She gave him The Joker's glare of disapproval. "Are you asking about my love life, Ben Tannen?"

"Well, I hadn't planned to, but the opening presented itself so..." He lifted a shoulder. She felt the flex of muscles through his sweater. "I could hardly say no."

"I see. Then, no." And, needing space, she slowed her steps.

Ben slowed his as well. "No?"

"No. No boy talk. No sweet nothings."

"A part of me finds that hard to believe. A part of me isn't surprised."

"A part of *me* finds that insulting. But since we're being totally honest here, I'm not surprised you feel that way." She smiled with her eyes. "Quentin and I may have been best friends, but you did know me better than anyone."

He didn't say anything for a minute, just slowed the dance until they were barely moving, until they were standing still in each other's arms. His hand flexed in the small of her back and his eyes were too familiar, too knowing as they searched hers for the truth.

How could he have known her better than anyone and not know a thing about her now? Her heart was suddenly beating too fast in a body that was too close to Ben's. *Showtime*, she thought and right on cue Ben spoke.

"Is it time to be totally honest, Heidi?"

"What do you mean?"

"C'mon. Let's get a drink," Ben said, taking her by the arm. He guided her toward the bar and chose two stools in the darkest corner.

Heidi was faced with hiking herself and her dress up onto the seat with Ben watching. She managed without exposing what shouldn't be exposed and didn't even lose the shoulder strap that began to slip as she settled.

Then Ben moved into her space in that very dark, very small corner.

"Beer?" he asked.

She nodded. She didn't want it, probably wouldn't drink it, but more than she needed to keep a clear head she needed something to do with her hands.

She was in a dark corner with Ben Tannen and he'd matured into more of a man than she'd been alone with since, well, ever.

He raised a finger and signaled the bartender who returned with a basket of peanuts, two longnecks and one frosted mug which he sat before Heidi. She poured slowly, letting the head build along with the tension.

Finally. The moment of truth. This is why she was here, wasn't it? To make things right with Ben?

The injury she'd inflicted had left a permanent scar on her memories of the past as thoroughly as it had on Ben's jaw. She needed to go through this...healing process.

It was a case of getting on with things, because until this very moment, sitting here next to Ben, his presence larger than life, she hadn't finally realized that she'd lived every day of her adult life waiting for this reunion.

"He's good, isn't he?"

"Hmm? Oh, Jack," she said, following the direction of Ben's gaze, watched Jack close his eyes and make the music come alive. "He is. I had no idea he kept playing after high school. Or that he'd stayed in the area."

"He left for a while," Ben said, cracking open a peanut. "School, then the military."

"Really? I didn't know."

He tossed the hull to the cement floor, tossed the meat into his mouth. "No reason you would have."

"That's true," she settled on saying. Why explain to Ben the reasons she hadn't kept in touch with a single one of her four best friends when she had yet to explain that to herself? "What does he do now? When he's not playing oldies in local clubs."

Ben laughed. "Seems strange calling these songs oldies. If they're oldies then I must be old and I'm not quite ready to admit to that."

"Hmm. If you were old I would be old and Jack would be old. I know I'm not. And Jack can't be, or he wouldn't be able to manage half those moves he's making up there. Whatever he does, he stays in shape."

"Once a military man, always a military man. And I'm sure he'll be glad to know that you noticed." Ben tilted his longneck Heidi's way for emphasis, then brought the bottle to his lips.

Heidi narrowed her eyes and glared. "Well, I can't help but notice. He's worked up a sweat and that T-shirt isn't exactly heavy-weight cotton." Nice, Heidi. Dig yourself in deeper. "So, what? Was he Army? Navy? Marines?"

"Marines. Now he's a special envoy of some sort." Ben chipped at the label on his bottle. "I'm sure he'll tell you what he can."

"Ooh. A man with secrets. I keep hearing rumors that this is supposed to be an interesting weekend." She pressed her thumbprint into the frost of her mug, enjoying a bit of satisfaction at having spread the rumor. "Maybe it will be."

Ben's eyes glittered in the light from the neon bar signs. "What were you expecting from this weekend?"

Now, that was a loaded question. How honest should she be? Should she admit she hadn't thought much at all about the actual reunion? That her only purpose in coming was to take care of what should've been settled years ago?

No. That would be too much, too soon. She'd just follow his lead, let him set the tempo and the tone of their private assignation.

"I expected to do a lot of sitting on the sidelines. Maybe earn my own case of benchwarmer butt." Ben smiled at that and she added, "I don't have a lot of catching up to do, you know."

"I might have to argue with that, counselor."

Smarty-pants. "Let me rephrase. I don't have a lot of old friends whose lives I need to catch up on."

"I can think of at least four."

"The same four I came to see," she said, lying through her teeth. She'd come to see one. She just wasn't ready to let him know that.

"I've kept up with you, you know." He dropped the bomb, then reached for his beer, letting Heidi deal with the explosive aftershock as he sipped.

"You have?" she asked, surprised, pleased, pleasured. And troubled. Why would Ben keep up with her?

She was the one with amends to make and she hadn't even known the major changes he'd gone through in downsizing his life-style. "Do you mind telling me why?"

He shrugged, his yellow sweater beautifully contouring his wide shoulders. "Never managed to let go of that big brother complex, I guess."

Thud. Heidi's heart hit her stomach and both fell to

her feet. Here she'd been wondering why he held her so close while they danced when he must've been trying to keep her out of the type of trouble she'd found so often in school.

She nodded. "You thought of me as a sister. I see."

"That was about as close as you'd let anyone get, Heidi."

She had to think about that for a minute, then supposed in a way he was right. Allowing anyone into her heart would've meant less room for the things that mattered most, at the time.

Besides, how would she have been able to leave if someone—anyone—had given her a reason to stay?

Heidi sighed. "Well, Ben. I never thought our relationship went beyond that of friends, but a sister..."

"It was a safe distance."

"You felt you had to keep your distance?"

Ben turned to face her, bar stool to bar stool. "Look what happened when I got too close," he said and met her gaze straight on.

She tried, truly tried not to look at the scar running the length of his jaw. She tried to hold his gaze, to hold onto the present, to keep the moment from sliding into the memories.

And she thought she'd done a fairly good job until Ben blinked, slowly raising long dark lashes to reveal the eyes of the boy she'd known, hated, admired, envied, and more.

She sighed. "We need to talk, don't we?"

Ben looked at her then, and while Heidi was struggling to breathe, he scooted forward on his bar stool and dug deep in his pocket. He pulled out a piece of paper, worn and folded.

Then he placed it flat on the bar, out in the open for everyone to see.

Of course no one but Heidi could know the truth and the pain of what was written, handwritten with purple ink, inside the folds.

And the fact that Ben still had it...fifteen years later and he still had it...

Memories sucked Heidi into the silt of the past. She felt the weight of the bicycle chain in her palm, felt the weight of hopeless desperation on her shoulders.

She saw again the check Ben held out to her, a simple draft—the terms of which couldn't have been more complicated in Heidi's mind.

He'd offered her money, a chance to start her education and she'd taken it, tying herself irrevocably to all that she'd condemned and hated about the Tannen way of life.

That day she'd lost the pride she'd held on to for four years, a pride that had kept her from believing what she knew was said about her—that she didn't belong, wasn't good enough, shouldn't forget where she came from.

Where she came from was coming back to haunt her now. Damn Ben for being her ghost.

He had an elbow propped on the bar and was staring at the paper square, twirling it with one index finger, spinning it around and around, drawing Heidi into the whirlpool of movement.

She felt fifteen years of confidence drain, leaving her with The Joker's arsenal of survival instincts. But The Joker now had the backbone of the Mighty Heidi Malone, which was an almost terrifying combination of moxie and mouth.

So, he had the nerve to silently threaten her with a moment of weakness that was fifteen years old? Fine, she'd turn his tables and dump the cards in his lap.

She pinned the note to the bar with one red nail. "Looks like you don't want to talk."

He cast her a sideways glance. The corner of his mouth lifted, deepening the dimple in his cheek. It was a smile, but he wasn't grinning. "I'm not sure you're up for the conversation I want to have."

"Now, Ace," she crooned, sliding off her bar stool and stepping close. She tossed her hair with the shrug of one shoulder, placed one hand on Ben's thigh. "You have no idea what I'm up for."

"That so?" he asked.

Nodding, she let the other hand trace the length of the scar she'd given him. It cut through the shadow of beard on his face the way she wanted to slice through his smug attitude.

So she leaned forward and, for the first time in her life, placed her mouth on his.

4

DAMN, THE WOMAN COULD KISS.

The touch of her fingers along his jaw was hard enough to take. Her hand on his thigh was hell. But what her mouth was doing to his mouth...

Damn, the woman could kiss.

Her lips were silky soft as she gently rubbed them against his. The tip of her tongue moistened a warm trail first over his top lip then down along the bottom. Her wet and tender touch was the most erotically innocent contact he'd ever shared with a woman.

Ever.

And this was Heidi's mouth making wicked with his.

Ben gripped the neck of his beer bottle until the embossed glass rim left an imprint in the center of his hand.

His other hand had no such anchor and he found his fingers sliding into her hair—hair rich and thick and gorgeous to the touch and nothing like the bleached out scarecrow-straw of the style she'd worn in high school.

His palm cupped the back of her head and held her where he wanted her. Oh, yeah. He wanted her. In ways dangerous for a man to want a woman. Dangerous when the lure was forbidden, the temptation unknown.

But it was primarily due to the forbidden temptation of being with this woman, the same Heidi who'd intrigued him for far too long. Her allure had escalated over the past fifteen years, taking on the nature of a fantasy in his very down-to-earth thirty-three-year-old mind.

He kissed her back. It was easy to do. He tilted his head, pressed forward and caught her unawares. She gasped, a brief sound and briefer parting of lips, but Ben knew how to play. His tongue slipped boldly into her mouth.

He wouldn't have held her and kissed her against her will, but she put up no struggle. She melted against him like a lover—or so it seemed. Her body hadn't moved, hadn't outwardly responded in any way. But he felt her consent in the caress of her breath on his mouth.

Ben had enough conscious sense left to realize that no matter what *he* was experiencing they weren't creating a whisper-causing spectacle here in the dark corner of the club. At least, not yet. A good thing considering that half the club had been waiting to see them in action. And action wouldn't be long in coming if Heidi kept up this kiss.

For now, though, the spectacle was all in his mind. Or in his mouth and rapidly moving lower. Heidi's tongue met every indecent, illicit advance his made.

He wanted to make love to her body. He wanted to feel her mouth on his skin and her tongue against his flesh. He wanted to strip her bare and take her fast, then watch her dress before removing her clothes slowly with his fingers. Exploring her the way her mouth was begging him to explore.

She kissed him more deeply, moaned low in the deepest part of her throat and moved her hand. The one on his thigh. She slid it upward along the material of his slacks until her fingers hit a roadblock.

She froze. He released her. She stepped back. Her face was nicely flushed. Even in the dim light, the color on her cheeks was high enough to see.

But it was the fire burning in her eyes that caught his attention, grabbed hold of his libido and wouldn't let go. She shook her head, then shook off most of the signals she was broadcasting, signals his pulsing antennae had no trouble receiving.

"Well, Ace. It feels like you *are* up for more than I am." She blew out a less than steady breath, pulled in another. "Tell ya what. I'm going to visit the little girls' room, then we can get back to talking about having that talk."

She eased out from between the bar stools and backed away from the bar. Her smile was the one The Joker had tossed off when she was in over her head. It struck Ben then how often that had happened, and how Heidi had always managed to survive.

This time she seemed different. Shaky. Like she wasn't sure how well she was going to snap back. He nodded, watched her go. She disappeared into the back hallway and he slumped forward. Both elbows propped on the bar, he braced his forehead on the heels of his hands and stared into the basket of peanuts.

What had just happened? What was that kiss all about? What was his brain doing in his pants? He'd planned to confront Heidi this weekend. She was the reason he was here. What he hadn't counted on was the way she'd reacted. To him.

He made her nervous, a truth she would have denied if he'd pressed. But she was right when she said that he'd known her better than anyone.

Which is why he knew she'd kissed him to throw him off balance, to counter what she perceived as a threat. The move still had him reeling.

When on the defensive, she was brilliant. She'd told him years before what direction she'd wanted to take her career. Her passion made for a persuasive argument and he'd never doubted she'd achieve her goal. He'd known, too, that her biggest obstacle was money.

He'd solved that problem for her and in the process created a host of new ones. The biggest being the chasm that one simple check carved between them.

Throughout their years of high school they'd had such a complicated relationship, richer than mere friends shared. It was deep and powerful and bonding. But it hadn't been love. Not then.

Not with his father and her mother and the pressures of band and the school newspaper, the yearbook, the Stingray he'd received for his seventeenth birthday and the off-limits sign she'd never let down.

At seventeen, he hadn't been ready to explore what brewed between him and Heidi. There'd been something... He'd seen it in her eyes. And he'd ruined it all by doing what a Tannen did and solving her problem with his money.

He'd been slow to snap, to understand how deeply her hurt ran. And why. But he'd understood, later, that *she* was the snob, the one who'd had the biggest problem with where she'd come from.

In the end, she hadn't returned either of his calls, or responded to his one invitation, making it clear that whatever had remained unspoken between them had dried up and blown away that day he'd bought and paid for her future.

And now he had the kiss to deal with. That kiss was not a reunion kiss or an old friend's kiss. He wasn't even sure it was a lover's kiss. He and Katherine had shared a nice passion. The same as he'd shared with women before and after.

But Heidi's kiss went beyond nice. And beyond passion. He wanted to know what that meant, what she wanted. Why she seemed to want it from him.

Whoever it was spreading the rumors was right. This was going to be a hell of an interesting weekend.

A slap on his back brought his head up.

"The music too much for you, Tannen?"

"Hey, Jack." Ben straightened on his stool, shook his bud's hand. "Taking a break already? Maybe the music's too much for *you*, old man."

"Not a chance. Besides, your problem isn't the music. In fact, your problem just headed to the powder room. You work fast, man. Who was that?" Jack raked back sweat-drenched hair, looked off toward the rear hallway.

Ben straightened, feeling more like himself and less like Heidi's leftovers. "You're kidding, right? You didn't recognize her?"

A shake of his head and Jack said, "Should I have? I wasn't exactly close enough to see any details."

"You saw enough," Ben grumbled.

"And I wasn't the only one. All the damn looks coming your way were throwing off my rhythm. Seems you and the lady had more of an audience than I did. And I haven't quite figured out why. I mean, it was a nice show, but it was just a kiss."

No. It wasn't just a kiss. In no way was it just a kiss. "The show wasn't drawing the spectators. The players were. Or at least the actress."

"So?" Slouched low on the stool, Jack waited. "Who *were* you locking lips with?"

Ben sat up for this one. Sat up and made sure he had the other man's attention. "Heidi Malone."

Jack's jaw dropped. He manually closed his gaping mouth. "No friggin' way! That was our joker?"

"And then some."

"I'll say, and then some. Thanks, man," he said to the bartender who'd set cool water in front of him. He swallowed, then turned back to Ben. "What happened to the punk hair, the Sid and Nancy look? What happened to the who-gives-a-crap attitude?"

Ben rolled his eyes. "Oh, she's still got an attitude. Trust me on that one."

"Uh-oh." Jack's gaze moved over Ben's shoulder. "I guess I'll have to since it doesn't look like I'm going to have a chance to see for myself."

"Whaddaya mean?"

"Your joker is moving toward the door." Raising the water glass for a second drink, he nodded in that direction. "The way she's walking I'd say she's on a mission from God."

"Well, hell." Ben pushed off his stool, dug in his pocket and tossed a ten onto the bar.

"I'd watch my back, Tannen." Jack got to his feet as

well. "Who knows what weapons she's packing. She came mighty close to cutting off your ear last time."

"It was my eye. Not my ear. Get back to playing your oldies, old man. Break's over." Giving Jack a backward wave, Ben headed for the door and for Heidi.

He'd never intended to finish all their business in one evening. He wasn't even sure the task could be managed in a weekend. But time had become a critical factor now that their business had moved from the past to the present.

He found her in the parking lot at the side of the club, unlocking the driver's door of a sporty luxury import. The low-slung model was black and shiny and classy. It fit Mighty Heidi well.

She turned her head his direction then, and the look in her eyes was so much of the girl he'd known, the child's eyes in the woman's face.

He wondered if she still felt like she had to keep herself separate. If she still, even at her level of success, considered herself an outcast.

He couldn't let himself believe that of her. Not after witnessing her at work tonight. Not when he knew the extent to which her clients and community adored her.

Not when he had plans to show her that success wasn't a license to desert one's friends, or forget the debts one owed.

He leaned an elbow on the car's roof and made sure she knew he wasn't moving. Made sure she knew he'd followed her outside intending to finish what she'd started in the bar.

Made sure he had her attention before he said, "Fifteen years later and we haven't made it out of the parking lot."

She tossed her purse to the passenger's seat then, still standing in the open door, turned to face him. "You know, I don't even know why I came here tonight."

He raised a brow. "Something about a high school reunion?"

"Oh, right. Silly me. And here I thought I'd been invited as the entertainment."

"Jack mentioned that. That he'd seen our show from the stage."

"Great." She started to pace forward, realized she had to walk past him to make any progress and stopped. "I am so sick of who noticed what and who mentioned that and who thinks this. Why can't anyone come up to me and just say what's on their mind?"

"Because they don't know who you are?" When she looked disbelieving, he added, "Jack had to ask."

"They know who I am." She bit off the words then deflated right before his eyes. Easing down into the driver's seat, she sat sideways in the open door. Her hands gripped the ivory leather seat on both sides of her hips. "Have I changed that much, Ben?"

"I think you're the best one to answer that, Heidi."

"I know I have a whole new look." Her fingers went to her head. "I let go of the bleach the first time I had to make a choice between my hair and another hour of study for an exam."

She gestured with both hands, as if the movement aided her thought process. "And makeup can make a big difference. I never wore any in high school, you know."

He hadn't known. Or, hadn't really thought about it. She'd always looked the way Heidi should look while he'd worn everything expected of him.

"I doubt it's the way you look as much as the No Trespassing sign you're still carrying. You never have made it easy for anyone to get to know you."

"You think it was easy for me, for any of the river kids, to go to school at Johnson? I did what I had to do to survive in your world, Ben." She lowered her voice, looked away. "And what I had to do to get out."

"You're not a river kid any more, Heidi."

Slowly, her head swung back his direction. Slowly, she uncrossed her legs and got to her feet. She straightened the strap on her dress at the same slow speed, her eyes never leaving his face.

"How do you know what I am? You have no idea what lies beneath the Mighty Heidi facade."

He laughed. He was liking this game. "You mean you can dress her up and take her out but she's still The Joker underneath?"

"I always *was* a big fan of playing dress-up."

Ben turned up the heat. "You were a big fan of undressing, too."

Her eyes flashed. "Count yourself lucky, Ace. You had a front row center seat for my one and only private strip show."

"Really? One and only?" That got him to thinking about the men who'd been in her life. "Are you a virgin, Heidi?"

"Would you like that? If I were?" She gave a tiny

snort. "Sexual experience. One more thing to have where I have not."

Of course she wasn't. He hadn't expected her to be. And this would be a lot more fun for the both of them without having to deal with the logistics of a first time.

"Is that all?" she prompted when he took too long to respond.

"You act like you're in a big hurry."

"It's a long drive to Dallas and I'd like to get on the road."

She was leaving. He should've known. "Running out on me again, huh?" He glanced through the windows into the lit interior of the car. "Maybe I should do a quick weapons check."

She clenched and released her fists and took a long steady breath before replying. "I don't have any weapons. I don't make a habit of assaulting people in parking lots, you know."

"I'm afraid your track record leads me to believe otherwise, counselor."

Heidi closed the car door and, arms across her chest, leaned back against it. She cast him a long sideways glance that captured all the frustration she was feeling. "So? Are we going to do this now? Here?"

"This? What do you mean by this?" He straightened, shoved his fists deep into his slacks pockets. "Are we going to stand out here in the parking lot all night talking? No. I don't think so."

"Where, then? Do you want to go back inside?"

"After that kiss?" He shook his head, shook off the lingering reminder of her mouth. "Why spoil all the speculation about what we're doing out here? The

talk has probably taken on a life of its own by now."
She grimaced and he changed the subject. "Where're
you staying?"

This time she shook her head. "I have a room at a
bed-and-breakfast, but I'm not staying."

Take it slow, he told himself then opened his mouth,
ignored his own sage advice, and jumped in. "Because of what just happened inside? Or because of
what happened fifteen years ago?"

She sighed her surrender. Facing the car, she
crossed her arms on the roof. Chin propped on her
wrists, she stared up into the starry June night.

"That's why I came, you know. Because of
the...assault." She looked his direction then, moving
to rest her cheek on her forearm. "And because of
you."

Ben pulled in a slow breath, almost forgot to ex-
hale. "You don't say?"

"Yes. I do say. We haven't even talked about it in
all this time. I mean, you tried." She was looking at
the sky again now. "I should've called you back.

"I just wasn't able or ready or old enough or whatever enough to deal with any of it. The money, the assault, it was all too much. And I was humiliated. Yes,
I needed the money. But it was so hard to take. Especially from you."

He knew what she said was true, though a lot of
years had passed before he understood the reasons.
He wanted to hear those reasons from her, now, and
he took a step closer.

"Why from me? It wasn't like I planned to send
Rocco and Bubba after you. I was surprised you paid
it back as quickly as you did. You didn't have to."

She backed away from the car. "What? You thought that because I lived on Deadbeat Drive and had the mother and the clothes and the future to show for it that I'd stiff you?"

Her voice had risen and she glared her displeasure. Her hands went to her hips. "You knew me better than that, Ben. I know you knew me better than that."

He was close enough now that, even with no light but that from the moon, he could see her rapid pulse where it beat at the base of her throat. The tiny black stones of her necklace shimmered as they rose and fell.

He liked the way they looked, not the way he seemed to be softening under her spell. He needed to remember why he'd come, remember the way she'd left him. "With the price I paid, I think I'd know you better."

Instead of the slap he'd expected her to deliver, she jerked open the car door. "Well, you just answered my one lingering question."

"What's that?"

"Whether or not you'd turn out to be a fine model of a Tannen." Her contemptuous gaze found his feet. "I see you've filled your father's shoes perfectly."

"My father's still wearing his own shoes, Heidi." It was time to see if she'd believe the truth. "What I've turned out to be has more to do with you than him."

"You're out of your mind, Ben. I haven't seen you for over a decade. If we'd stayed in touch and I'd kept you from burning brain cells by bingeing at frat keg parties, then you'd have a case. But you don't."

She rubbed at her forehead before looking up again. "Look, I came here to offer you an honest apology. I didn't expect forgiveness. But I did want to put an end to the silence."

"An end? And here I thought that kiss was just the beginning."

"Of what?" Her brows drew together. When he reached into his pocket, she waved off his intent with both hands. "Oh, no. Don't tell me you plan to hold me to that note. I can't even believe you still have it."

He looked at the square of paper from all sides. "It's a perfectly good IOU."

"Written under duress and therefore inadmissible."

"You're advising that I write it off as a bad debt?"

She nearly growled. "Ben. I was seventeen. I was at the end of my rope. I could've promised to deliver the moon and it would've been as empty a vow."

"But you didn't promise me the moon, Heidi." He stepped closer. "You promised me your body."

The tension didn't even have a chance to grow. Intruding footsteps came to a halt directly behind Ben. "Whoa. Did I just hear that right?"

Heidi pushed past Ben to link her arm through Quentin's. "Quentin. Hi. And, no. You didn't hear anything."

The relief in Heidi's expression was a burr under Ben's saddle. He looked from her pale face to Quentin's. The timing of the other man's arrival set Ben on edge. He'd wanted to finish his business with Heidi before she skipped town.

Still holding onto Heidi, Quentin slapped a too-friendly hand on Ben's shoulder. "Now, Ace. It sounds like you're putting the moves on our joker here? Take my advice. Give it up. Because I've already used every line I can think of and I am *still* reeling from the rejection."

He pretended to stumble. Heidi chuckled. Ben didn't even move. He hated the interruption when he was so close to getting to Heidi the way she'd gotten to him all these years.

But he finally had to shake his head. "You always did have perfect timing, Marks."

"Not timing, Ben. Rhythm." Quentin clicked rhythmic fingers. "Don't forget. I'm a professional. Which is why I'm out here sticking my nose in places it doesn't belong. I'm afraid business is about to cut short my weekend. And I'd really like to spend the rest of my time here in the company of friends."

He arched a brow. "And if one of those friends is a hell of a sexy woman, all the better. You still in the mood for that burger, Heidi? Ben? You want to join us?"

Quentin's gaze passed between them until Ben gave up all hope of getting back to business. He propped a hip against the rear quarter panel of Heidi's car. "Heidi was just leaving."

"What? She can't be just leaving. She just got here. Besides," he continued, looking straight at Heidi. "I'm not going to be able to stay until Sunday. We only have tonight and tomorrow morning to catch up."

"I don't know, Quentin." Her indecision was the perfect cover for finding an excuse to turn him down. "I have a big case coming to trial week after next. I really shouldn't have even taken off this one night."

"C'mon, Heidi. We've only had fifteen minutes. That hardly makes up for fifteen years." When she still looked unconvinced, Quentin compromised. "At least stay for tomorrow's picnic. Then if you're still feeling the need to leave, I'll let you drive me to the airport on your way out."

Ben stood back and let Quentin do all the work. It went against his grain to do so, but it was so entertaining to watch Heidi's conflicting emotions.

She knew if she stayed he'd want to pick this up where they'd just left off. And that bothered her as much as the short black dress she'd been fighting all night.

Besides, he was curious about her loyalties, if she'd really come here for the apology she hadn't gotten around to. If she'd come here for him, as she'd said.

Decision made, she shook back her curls. "Tell ya what. Let's go eat. I can't make any promises on an empty stomach. Feed me and I'll do anything."

"Great. Now she tells us," Quentin grumbled. He took a closer look at her car, whistled when he saw the make and model. "Nice. But this baby ain't gonna hold the three of us. How 'bout it, Ben? You got more room? Or you want me to call a cab?"

Ben bowed out. He didn't have a problem letting Heidi stew, because he knew without a doubt that she'd stay. "You two go on. I need to get home. I have a pregnant mare to see to."

His out-of-the-blue announcement worked. Heidi extricated herself from her protector and approached. The curiosity in her eyes could've killed a half-dozen cats. "Horses? You have horses?"

Yeah. This was going to work out fine. "And a half-dozen cats. And even one ragged old dog."

"You're kidding. Where do you live?"

"Tomorrow," he said and backed away.

"Blackmailer." He half expected her to stick out her tongue.

"You were closer to the mark earlier, you know."

"How so?"

No matter what effect she'd had on his life, the truth was still the truth. "I'm a Tannen. Still my father's son."

5

Freshman year

"WHAT IN THE HELL IS THAT?"

Adjusting the strike of his bass drum pedal, Ben deliberately didn't look up. Randy'd been distracting the rest of the group with some lamebrain deal or another since seventh grade.

But this was high school. The competitions would mean a lot more now.

And focusing on practice, not to mention finding a replacement for their saxophonist who'd moved to Corpus Christi over the summer, deserved more attention than Randy, the proverbial boy who cried wolf.

So it took Jack's, "I don't believe it," and Quentin's, "She'd better know how to play that thing," to break Ben's concentration and draw his attention to the practice room doorway.

He'd seen her once or twice in the band hall during summer registration, figured she was one of the kids who'd gone to the junior high down by the river. For years there'd been a campaign calling for a redistricting of Johnson High's lines. The circulating petitions ranted about tax issues.

Right. Like the few river kids attending JHS really put a drain on the funds.

He wished the crusading parents—his included—would just get over it. So what if rich kids and poor kids went to the same school? This girl didn't look like she was any happier about where she came from than he was.

He pushed up from behind the bass drum and watched her enter the room, stop, close the door behind her. She wore what looked like a man's pinstriped suit pants. With work boots that were a matching dark brown. On top of chopped-off hair the color and consistency of hay, she'd mashed a man's brown hat.

The interesting part was what she wore between the hat and the pants. It looked like underwear. Or those nightie things girls slept in. It barely came down to the waist of the pants.

It was black and shiny, with thin straps holding it up on her shoulders. And he could see a lot of her bra, lace and ribbons and stuff, like maybe she was going for a Madonna look or something.

She was tall and sorta scrawny, but in a curvy sort of scrawny way. And she had the biggest darkest eyes, with lashes that made him think of *A Clockwork Orange*. Or maybe they just looked that way because her face and all of her skin was so pale.

In one hand she held a book satchel and a horn case. In the other she held a saxophone that had long since lost its brass sheen.

It looked like they'd found their fifth.

"Hey," she said to the room. Her gaze traveled from Ben to Randy to Jack to Quentin and back. She looked at him for a very long time, or it seemed like a long time, because of the way she was looking.

It was weird to say, but she made him feel as if they were the only two people in the room. And that made him feel like a real dork. He would've understood it better if she'd looked at him the way girls had looked at him since fourth grade. But it wasn't like that.

She wasn't batting her lashes or pouting her lips. She wasn't checking him out. It was like she didn't see the uniform of his social circle, the button-fly 501 jeans, the untied high-top sneakers, the turned-up collar and green alligator logo on his yellow shirt. And it made him wonder what, instead, she saw.

The whole scene turned into a weird freeze-frame. No one moving. Just these five people squared off in four-to-one odds in this drab cold room with industrial-strength floors and acoustical ceiling tiles.

"Hiya." Quentin finally raised his hand, stood up from his piano bench. She waved the fingers holding her case, but didn't say anything else. "I'm Quentin. Marks."

"I'm Heidi. Malone," she answered.

Jack was next. He plucked two strings on his standing bass. "Jack Montgomery."

Never taking her eyes off Jack, she raised her horn, licked her lips and blew a quick two notes. The same quick two notes. "Heidi Malone."

Ben grinned to himself and waited Randy's turn. Randy glanced over and shrugged, turned back to the waif standing alone with her back to the door.

He walked toward her a couple of steps, gestured with his trumpet. "Randy Schneider. I hope Mr. Philips knows what he's doing, sticking us with you."

Ben grimaced. Randy and his big mouth. But she seemed to take it in stride.

"Heidi Malone," she said. "And I hope he knew what he was doing by sticking me with you four."

Randy turned away, blew a puff of breath into the trumpet's mouthpiece. "Weird chick," he mumbled under his breath as Ben walked up to bat.

He jumped off the small platform, tossed back his hair. "Heidi Malone. Hi, I'm Ben Tannen."

"Hi, Ben," she said almost for his ears alone.

"Hey. Listen. You gotta know this is our third year to play together. The four of us." He jerked his chin back, indicating the other three who were keeping their distance. "It's gonna be like a weird adjustment to get used to—"

"Playing with a girl?"

Randy choked on his laughter. Jack snorted. Quentin rolled his eyes, turned, banged his forehead against the piano.

Ben tried to keep a straight face and an open mind. "No. To get used to a new sax player." He nodded toward her horn. "You do know how to play that thing, don't you?"

"I can play."

Randy offered the first challenge. "Prove it."

Heidi moved to set her shabby leather satchel and horn case on the same round table where the others had piled their books. "Boys," she said to no one in particular. "Always after girls for proof."

Ben crossed his arms and propped one hip on the table. From the stage platform behind him he heard sniggers and under-the-breath gutter remarks. He was sure Heidi heard them, too, but she went on as if the comments were nothing.

She cast but a cursory glance in the direction of the other three before Ben received her full attention. "What do you want? David Sanborn? Clarence Clemmons? Charlie Parker?"

Quentin's head popped up. He walked closer. "You know Charlie Parker?"

Heidi arched a brow over one big dark eye. "You know Scott Joplin?"

The smile Quentin gave Ben wasn't quite as shaky as before and was the first sign of the afternoon that maybe they weren't screwed after all. Ben shrugged, nodded at Heidi to go ahead.

She stood still, both feet flat on the floor, fingers with chewed-up nails poised over keys. Taking a deep breath, she managed a very clean, very precise, very bland first few bars of the national anthem.

Randy flopped to the floor and groaned. Jack gripped the neck of his bass and shook his head. Quentin's mouth pulled into a grim line. Ben figured by the time she hit *the home of the brave* Quentin would've reached the door to Mr. Philips's office to raise holy hell.

There was no real reason to wait that long. Might as well put everyone out of their misery now.

Ben eased off the table to stop Heidi's really bad audition, but never made it another step because she held the high note over *the rocket's red glare* and then began to move. And to play. To really, really play.

It was amazing to watch, amazing to listen to. She had her eyes closed, screwed up tight one minute, brows lifted high the next, getting into the song like it was what she lived for. Every note dead on. She knew exactly what she was doing.

And he didn't doubt for a minute that she'd done what she'd done on purpose. She was taking their measure the same as they'd taken hers. Not only had they found their fifth, they'd met their match.

The song she played wasn't familiar to Ben, but Jack had no trouble picking up the tempo. He thrummed the strings of his bass, *bdmp-bmp-bmp*, *bdmp-bmp-bmp-bmp*. Ben found his own foot counting the beat. *Bdmp-bmp-bmp, bdmp-bmp-bmp-bmp*.

He crossed the room, picked up his sticks and lightly struck the skin of the snare. He smiled when he saw Quentin give up the fight and not even bother with the piano bench, standing instead while he banged out accompanying chords.

Randy looked from Heidi to each of the others and back. His head was moving, both in rhythm and in disbelief. He finally let out a loud, "Yeowza! Quentin, my man. You are on your way."

The music fizzled. Heidi was the last to stop playing. She met the eyes of each boy, lingering longest on Ben, before she walked to the table and picked up her things.

"I expect each of you to be here after school tomorrow. Three-thirty sharp."

And then she left the room. Ben watched her go. And then he just cracked up.

It was going to be an interesting four years.

He wondered if they'd all survive.

THE SHORT CORRIDOR bisecting the small barn smelled like hay and early morning. And like impending birth. Ben stopped at the last stall in the short row of three. He hooked his arms over the swinging door's top slat and looked from the quivering mare to the man checking her progress. "How's she doing?"

Thackery Jones took his time, moving in low third gear—the only speed Ben had seen the older man move since he'd hired on four years ago. The slow motion had nothing to do with age and everything to do with precision.

Which was exactly the reason Ben had chosen him and now depended on him to oversee the daily operation of the place. In his sixty-two years, Thackery had forgotten more about the ins and outs of country living than Ben would ever learn.

The older man didn't rush with the mare, staying where he was until he'd finished his business and found the horse's progress to his liking. Only then did he push up from a bending position in denim jeans as broken in as the leather of both his belt and his boots.

He spoke softly and in dulcet tones, making his unhurried way toward the animal's low-hanging head. The words he next spoke to Ben were carried on the same even breath. "The way it's lookin', you'll be a daddy by the time you get back from Sherwood Grove tonight."

A living, breathing expansion of his holdings. His very first—since he didn't count the cats who ran from the field to the barn these days in what seemed like small herds. He was finally getting there, settling into a deep state of satisfaction with his life.

Funny how the birth of a horse that couldn't even weigh a hundred pounds and had only the barest value as a capital asset could put a smile on his face. He could only imagine what sort of look it would put on his father's.

He laughed, but kept the sound in the back of his throat. "Don't be bringing my bloodlines into it. I'm afraid they've caused me enough trouble already."

The one brow Thackery lifted was grizzled and gray. "You saw your little girl last night, did you?"

Ben debated on telling Thackery how much of a little girl Heidi had ceased to be. "I saw her. Danced with her. Fought with her. Kissed her."

Thackery laughed softly, the sound a veritable lullaby, his wide smile white against his smooth dark skin. "You two sound about as chummy as me and Mrs. Jones."

He and Heidi? Chummy? Didn't that paint an interesting picture. "Now, that thought's enough to keep me home today. You sure you don't need a hand with Charlie here?"

"And which of your hands you plannin' to give? That right one there that spends all day cuttin' and pastin'? Or the left one that's busy checking voice mail and speed dialing? No *sirree*." Thackery pushed out his bottom lip and shook his head. "If I need a hand, I'll be wanting Doc Specter's."

Charlie wuffled at the sound of the vet's name and both men turned their heads. This horse had a special place in Ben's heart. He wanted her to have the best care. "Should I call the Doc?"

Thackery whispered calming words to the horse. "Charlie's fine. All she needs is peace and quiet and a clean bed of hay to be droppin' this foal on. She don't need the Doc. And she sure don't need your nervous Nelly fidgeting."

Ben hadn't thought he was fidgeting until Thackery nodded toward the silver watchband Ben was stretching and turning inside out and back again.

He settled it back on his wrist and stepped away from the stall door. "Maybe I'll just hang around today."

Thackery reassured Charlie and gave her nose a soothing stroke before he eased open the swinging door and joined Ben in the corridor. The stall's latch made the barest click as it caught. "I don't know why. You're not exactly dressed for a delivery."

Thackery was right on that one. Denim shorts, athletic shoes and a white polo shirt wouldn't stand up to the rigors of an animal birth. "Only a city boy would attend a birth in picnic attire, right?"

"Attire? Only a city boy would talk like a...well, a city boy. But at least you ain't stupid enough to've married yourself to concrete." His legs bowed but strong, Thackery headed for the tack room, adding over his shoulder, "At least you found enough good sense to bring you out this way."

The other man walked off, leaving Ben to ponder or follow. He did both. "Maybe good sense is what kept me in Denver. Could've been insanity that brought me out here."

In the beginning, while trading in the luxury car for a truck, custom-tailored suits and Italian leather loafers for off-the-rack blue jeans and cowhide boots, he'd wondered what had gotten into him. He wondered less often lately.

"Well, good sense is keeping you here now."

Thackery picked up an awl and a stirrup leather, gestured toward Ben with the pointed end of the piercing tool. "Good sense and Mrs. Jones's cooking, that is."

Ben grabbed hold of his flat abs and jiggled. "Mrs. Jones's cooking is going to make it impossible for me to leave. Except in a dump truck."

Thackery shook his head without ever looking up from the leather strip. "A wheelbarrow maybe. You won't be needin' a dump truck for at least ten more years."

"By the end of the day I'll need one or the other. Do you know how long it's been since I've swung a tennis racket?" He swung an imaginary racket and winced only once.

"What're you worried about? You ain't exactly a marshmallow, even if you do sit behind a desk most of the day."

"I don't do much sitting these days. Not with running that one-man newspaper show. And not with you keeping me hopping every minute that I'm home." He swung the racket again. Better. A little stretching and he'd be fine.

"Look here, city boy. You want to be a gentleman rancher you can't just be polite and sit up straight when you ride Miss Charlie. You gotta do some of the ranching for it to take."

"Gentleman rancher, huh? I'm not sure this place qualifies as a ranch."

That grizzled gray brow came up again. "What would you call it?"

Ben shrugged. That was easy. "Home."

Thackery hung the awl on its hook. "Well, your

home's got some ranching that needs to be done. And since you plan to spend your day playing with a ball that ain't even a ball, I'd better get to making hay."

Ben couldn't resist. "I thought we bought our hay."

"City boy," Thackery grumbled and headed out of the barn, stirrup leather in hand.

Ben shook his head and watched his good friend go. After closing on the property in Stonebridge, the first thing he'd looked for was a caretaker. *The Stonebridge Reporter* hardly operated at the pace of *The Denver Post*, but Ben's duties as publisher kept him busy enough that he'd known he'd need help maintaining his new place.

What he didn't know was which decision had been the smartest—buying the property or hiring the Jones couple.

Thackery and Mrs. Jones were a perfect team. Mrs. Jones ran the household. Thackery took care of the buildings and grounds, freeing up Ben's time to devote to the paper. The townspeople deserved a first-class publication and knowing he had the Joneses taking care of business at home allowed Ben to make it one.

Giving Thackery a final wave, Ben turned back into the barn and stopped by Charlie's stall again. She returned his stare, slowly blinking those big brown eyes. "Hey, girl. It won't be long now."

She'd been his first livestock purchase, this horse, once he'd moved into the rambling two-story house. The ratty-looking dog just showed up under the front porch one day and the cats...who knew where they came from. And came from. And came from.

Owning a horse had never been a dream he'd entertained. Owning a ranch, though ten acres hardly qualified, and being a gentleman rancher had never been his grand plan. He'd known he needed a change. He'd returned to Sherwood Grove and the Austin area for a family visit, seen what was happening in Stonebridge and felt the stirrings of his first real roots.

The funny thing was, plan or not, the scaling down to this slower pace left him feeling incredibly settled. Up until making this move, he'd done more of what was expected of a Tannen than what he expected of himself.

In the beginning, he'd avoided all but the most benign teen rebellion and angst and had come of age without sit-ins or walk-outs. Economic depression had taken the fire out of protests. No one could afford the time or energy.

No one but those who lived like the Tannens.

He'd enjoyed working on the *Johnson High Journal* and heading up the yearbook staff. Continuing his studies in journalism had been a natural extension of that interest. He even counted his choice of university as his own, though he'd been expected to attend University of Texas, as all Tannens did.

Once married, Katherine's rising star had been the impetus for most of their moves. He hadn't objected to the relocations, easily climbing to the top in his own editorial field. Who wouldn't want a Tannen on staff, after all?

Katherine had cultivated their circles of friends, furnished their homes without his input. She'd had exquisite taste in people and place settings—even if the former strangely mirrored his father's, the latter reflecting his mother's.

So, it wasn't surprising that he'd felt as if he were living someone else's life, fulfilling the expectations into which he'd been born, the very expectations into which Katherine had married.

His dissatisfaction, in fact, had been slow in its evolution. The changes to his way of thinking, his way of seeing the world around him, had in no way come about overnight.

But Katherine had noticed and had left—she didn't need his name and influence any longer, she'd said. She certainly didn't need his obvious disinterest, she'd added. He hadn't been fair to her, no, but she'd married the father's son, expecting him to be the father.

Expectations had ruled too much of his existence. To an outsider he had a perfect life. But his perfect life had no heart or soul. And Heidi's assault had caused him to see that.

He'd been honest when he'd told her last night of the effect she'd had on who he was today. It had taken a trip home to Sherwood Grove after his breakup with Katherine, Ben's first visit in several years, to see that he needed to cut the Tannen ties.

To see clearly for the very first time, through the eyes and ears of an adult, of an equal, that his family bought and sold people as often as they did product. That they used money to cover a multitude of sins, and as an easy fix. How simple it was to grease a palm rather than work toward an honorable solution.

Exactly what he'd done with Heidi.

Heidi had been the one to live with the humiliation

of his Tannen-like gesture, while he'd gone on to UT with only the scar on his face.

He'd wondered then if, once on their own and away from prying parental eyes, they might explore those unexplored years of tension. She'd answered that by not returning either of his calls.

He wondered now if her hurt had fueled her success, if she'd been driven to prove that his name and family position meant nothing.

He wondered how far he could take that purple-printed IOU promise of her body. And if she really had the experience her voice had claimed, or was still the virgin he'd seen in her eyes.

The horse in front of him blew out a shuddering breath, bringing him back to the present. "I know, girl. I know. The waiting'll be over soon." He backed away from the stall to go.

"I'll see you tonight, Miss Charlie Parker."

6

THE LAST TIME she'd found herself at a picnic table in this particular park, Heidi had been holding a check in her hand. A large check, more money than she'd ever seen at one time in her young life.

She hadn't known a single seventeen-year-old who'd had a checking account. She shouldn't have been surprised to find a seventeen-year-old named Tannen would have one. What did surprise her was finding out Ben had the amount of money he did.

She'd known his family was wealthy, of course. But to have so much money of his own...money for clothes, a car, even gas for his car. Dang it. She'd been so naive, had *so* underestimated how out of his league she was.

From her position at the far edge of the park, her denim-covered bottom on a weathered tabletop, her sneaker-soled feet on the scarred and splintered bench, Heidi watched the reunion organizers pull together long tables bearing food and coolers of iced drinks, watched their children unload bats and gloves, tennis rackets, Frisbees and volleyballs from the back ends of minivans and SUVs.

Damn that Quentin Marks for sweet-talking her into staying. Their one-on-one visit had lasted late into the night. She'd enjoyed the time, had demanded his phone number before they'd done much more than order their food because she realized on the drive to the diner how much she'd missed his candor—and his ability to see through her bullshit.

It had taken but one, "Tell me the truth, Heidi," to get her talking about her past and her present with Ben. Over the course of the evening, Quentin had learned everything—about the assault and the note, the debt she'd repaid and the one Ben had reminded her of last night.

She just wished she'd been strong enough to tell Quentin no, that they couldn't pick up last night's conversation this morning, that she had to leave first thing. That she couldn't afford to take time for today's picnic and certainly not for the country club dance tonight.

She needed to be home in Dallas, poring over legal briefs, filling yellow legal pads with copious notes. That was the life she understood. The life she'd worked so hard to attain. The late nights, early mornings, little-time-to-sleep and less-time-to-eat life of the Mighty Heidi Malone.

At this moment, she couldn't have felt any less like Mighty Heidi and any more like The Joker. A part of that had to do with being here in this park with the people who'd known her only as the one and not the other.

But more than anything what she was feeling had to do with Ben. And how one evening in his presence seemed to have rendered null and void the steps she'd taken to reach her level of success—success worthy of a Tannen.

He'd stood there in the parking lot at The Cave, his

eyes glittering in the light from the moon, his dark hair windblown, the scar on his face slashing through the shadow of his beard, the lips she'd kissed moving, speaking words with the voice that had soothed her old misery, and she'd wanted to run screaming into the night.

She'd felt as if her life was a masquerade, that what she'd achieved was all a farce, that she'd never measure up. And that beneath one coordinating foundation-to-accessory ensemble costing more than her four-year Johnson-High wardrobe, she still wore the harlequin mask that had served her so well.

She hated feeling like a fraud, that all she'd accomplished since leaving Ben in that parking lot meant nothing, when she knew, dammit, she *knew* she'd made a colossal difference in the lives of the women she'd counseled and represented.

How could one man do this to her? Make everything seem like nothing, so much like so little? She turned her head, physically avoiding what she didn't want to answer. Because her heart of hearts knew this was personal. This was more than Ben. This was the reason she'd avoided Sherwood Grove and her four best friends for the past fifteen years.

This had to do with where she'd come from and the escape she'd made, never having come to grips with the legacy she was leaving behind. She should have listened to Georgia. She shouldn't have come. She should, instead, have gone blindly forward with the rest of her life and forgotten she'd ever heard the name Tannen.

The wooden table shifted and creaked and Heidi looked over to see Jack Montgomery settling onto the opposite end. He wore sunglasses and a T-shirt similar to the one he'd played in last night, but he'd traded his biker boots for athletic shoes and his jeans for gray sweats cut off at the knees.

He sidled an inch or two closer, nudged his shades down his nose and peered over the rims. His green eyes burned with a fire that rivaled the intensity of Ben's. "Someone told me you're Heidi Malone. But I couldn't be sure seeing as last night all I saw was your exit."

"A little bird tells me that's not quite all you saw." Heidi decided to wait for a cue from Jack about his mood before saying more. His expression was unreadable. And she preferred to avoid a repeat of the emotional hot water she'd jumped into with Ben last night.

Jack removed his sunglasses completely, tossed them to the table, scooted another couple of inches closer. "True. I did see more. But I've learned through the years that discretion is the better part of valor."

Gripping the tabletop with both hands, Heidi looked into Jack's eyes. Funny how with this man as well as Quentin, she didn't see as much of the boy she'd known as she'd seen looking deep into Ben's eyes.

Damn. If this weekend got any deeper, she'd need to scrounge up a pair of waders. Better yet, overalls and barn boots. "So...if I don't mention what we're not talking about, you won't mention what we're not talking about?"

"We can do that." He moved another inch. And another. "Or..." he arched a brow "...we can blow that off and just go for it. Given the right incentive, I can forget everything I've ever learned about valor and discretion and get down and dirty like you can't imagine."

"I see." She fought back a grin. "What happens then?"

"Then, we get back to talking about you and Ben. And I say, 'What the hell took you two goats so long?'" He moved closer, this time a good half a foot.

Goats? "And what do you say if I tell you that I'm not Heidi?"

Jack grimaced.

Well, that looked ominous. "Go ahead. I can take it."

"Huh? Oh, I sure hope you're Heidi because I really don't want anyone else to know that I've been scooting across a wooden table wearing nothing but a jock and sweats and now I have a splinter the size of Tennessee in my butt."

Heidi laughed out loud as Jack jumped up off the table. He squirmed around, batting at his backside until Heidi waved him over. She got to her feet and ordered him to lean across the end of the table.

Jack narrowed one eye before bending. "What if Ben catches us? In the act?"

"So what if he does?" Heidi took a long look at Jack's jersey-covered rear before shaking herself back to the moment at hand. She reached for the tiny sliver of wood stuck more *to* his jersey sweats than *in* any portion of his anatomy.

"Whaddaya mean, 'So what?'" Jack straightened, rubbed at the sting and turned to catch Heidi staring. His grin belonged to the cockiest cock of the walk. "Hey, hey, hey. Eyes front and center."

A warm flush crawled up her cheeks. "I'm only examining my handiwork like any professional."

Jack obviously didn't buy it for a minute. "A legal doctor, eh? As opposed to a medical doctor? Can't say I've run across too many of those in my travels."

"You've been busy keeping up with my career as well, I see." Heidi crossed her arms over her chest.

"Me? No way. I've just been listening to Ben keep up with it."

Heidi felt like tapping an exasperated foot until Jack held open his arms and grinned. "C'mere, Heidi. Give the ol' Jackster a hug."

How could she resist? "Oh, Jack. It's so good to see you."

Feeling him wasn't half-bad either and taking in an eyeful had been downright great, though those thoughts were neither here nor there. "You were wonderful last night. I had no idea you'd gone on to play professionally."

He released her, laid a quick finger over her lips. "Uh-uh. None of that P-word. I play for fun. I sing for fun. I've been working big-time the last few years on puttin' fun back into my life."

"Ben told me you'd been in the Marines?"

"Can you believe it?" He shook his head, as if he had a hard time believing it himself. "We were all so paranoid in high school about Carter enacting the draft registration, and I end up enlisting. Go figure."

Heidi leaned back against the picnic table. "I guess you've seen a lot of the world."

"Yep. I have. Seen a lot of the world. All that I care to see."

The way he said it, biting off his words with a sudden burst of bitterness, raised questions Heidi didn't dare ask. "Ah, and now you're back to having fun."

"I call it a regret minimization framework. I don't want to hit eighty and wonder how I got there. Or what happened to the years in between." He snagged up his sunglasses from the table. "I figure if I take care of the fun, the rest will fall into place."

"And that philosophy is serving you well?"

"So far, so good. All I'm missing is the sort of fun you were having with Ben last night."

Heidi hesitated in her reply. She wasn't sure how much of this she wanted to get into with Jack—Ben's friend, Jack. Instead, she shoved her hands in her pockets and begin to walk the trail around the park's perimeter. Jack fell into step at her side.

"I wasn't exactly having fun with Ben last night," she finally said after they'd walked a minute in silence.

"That so."

She glanced up at Jack's grin, watched as he returned his shades to his face, wished she had a pair to hide behind. She certainly could've used a pair last night.

"What I mean is...fun is not what I was aiming for when I kissed him."

"You kissed him, huh?" Jack ducked to avoid a low-hanging branch. "Well, I don't know what you started out aiming for, but from where I stood it seemed you hit a bull's-eye of a good time."

A good time. That was certainly too simplistic, wasn't it? For what she'd felt while kissing Ben? A good time was dinner with Quentin. Or now, here, walking and talking to Jack.

But that kiss with Ben? She'd felt...movement. She didn't want to say it had been the earth. But all the way from her tongue to her toes there'd been a whole lot of shaking going on.

She warded off a shiver. "A good time? That's certainly an interesting reason to kiss someone."

"You must not've done a lot of kissin' in your time, Heidi Malone. Or you'd know there're a hundred reasons one body kisses another." Both eyebrows wiggled above the pewter rims of his sunglasses.

"I know plenty of reasons." She wasn't sure she knew a hundred—might even have trouble coming up with that many if pressed—but still. How dare Jack assume her experience to be so limited. "You kiss for friendship and affection and love—"

"And passion and lust and a good ol' building of body heat." When she snorted without so much as a hint of refinement, Jack laughed and added, "But there's not much point to any of those reasons if you're not having fun, get my drift?"

She didn't want to get his drift. "Okay. The kiss was...enjoyable. Fun even," she added when his frown pressed the point. "It's not like it meant any more than that." *Go ahead, Heidi. Perjure yourself while you're at it.*

"Hey, that's none of my business. What it meant is between you and Ben." He pointed one finger her direction. "Just don't forget what I said."

"I know. I know. Fun or bust," Heidi said and picked up the pace.

Jack matched her stride, kicking a pinecone cluster from the dirt path. "I'm just glad to see you two finally getting around to doing it."

Heidi stopped dead in her tracks. "I am not getting around to *doing* anything. All I'm *doing* is offering Ben a long overdue apology."

"Say what you will, sister." Jack stepped closer, towered over her. "What you laid on Ben fifteen years ago won't stay with him half as long as what you laid on him last night."

"That's ridiculous." Heidi looked away toward the picnic festivities, took a deep breath and looked back. "Fifteen years ago I scarred Ben for life."

"Glad to see I made my point. Now," he said, taking her hand and pulling her off the pathway while she tried to interpret his meaning. "They're choosing up teams on the field down there. Let's go play ball."

"GO, RANDY! Knock it out of the park!" Even with Julie's full-bodied encouragement, Randy, after a long 3-2 count, only managed to eke out a single. Julie shoved away from the chain-link fence and plopped back down on the dugout bench next to Heidi. "Man, they are killing us."

Heidi watched Jack pitch to the next batter. If he was having fun, it didn't show in his face, in his stance, or even in his attitude. He'd long since tossed off his T-shirt, and beneath his shades and sweat-drenched hair, his mouth was grim.

His accomplice in this game of win or die trying was having just as much fun. Squatting behind home plate, Ben caught every burner Jack hurled, shouting encouragement to his cohort and catcalls at the batters.

Heidi spared a glance Julie's way. "Killing us,

yeah. But look how much fun they're having doing it."

"You think those two planned this attack?" Julie nodded toward the dynamic bare-chested duo. "And who let them play on the same team, anyway?"

"I think that's what's called stacking the deck." Adjusting the brim of her baseball cap, Heidi squinted and, hands on knees, leaned forward, staring out into center field where Quentin pounded fist to glove waiting to snag his next fly ball.

Her gaze traveled back to the infield, where Randy had taken a dicey lead off first. She then focused on the pitcher's mound, on Jack as he prepared his windup, checking out Randy's big jump from the base.

Finally, she took a good long look at home plate, at the batter's box and the man crouched low behind. Ben had long since stripped off his white polo shirt and tied a blue bandanna around his forehead. Beneath denim shorts, his thigh muscles flexed as he balanced on the balls of both feet.

She just wished he hadn't taken off his shirt. Not that she'd never seen him shirtless. She had. Years ago...in high school...before he'd reached his broad-shouldered potential. Before his biceps bulged with the throw of a ball, before his back stretched with long straps of muscle.

Before a wedge of dark hair defined his chest and made her fingers itch to thread through it. Years ago in high school she'd been just one of the guys, which had made it hard to look her fill as she was doing now.

She stood, leaving Julie and the rest of the team on the dugout bench, and hooked her fingers through the chain links of the fence. Her gaze moved again, from the strong lines of Ben's back to Jack to Randy to Quentin.

Four men. Her four men. Friends who'd seen her through four years of high-school hell. Who'd kept her sane and focused and on time to class. Who'd made her see that a drunken mother wasn't the end of the world.

Four men who'd encouraged her to pursue her dream when she couldn't see beyond cigarette burns on linoleum flooring. Or the insects who shared her bathtub drain. Or the men who bought what her mother sold at a blue-light-special discount.

Four men. *Her* four men. *Friends* who'd believed in her. Friends who'd known that no one could make more of a difference than a river kid who'd survived life. One who'd sharpened both her tongue and her mind, and clawed her way out of the gutter.

Jack's next pitch struck the leather of Ben's glove with a sting as sharp as the tears in Heidi's eyes. She blinked hard. And again felt the stares. Again heard the whispers. Yet this time her sense of discomfort was lessened.

Because the deepest part of her knew that what she shared with her four men was rare. Rare enough to spawn speculation from those unable to fathom the bond of The Deck. Rare enough to incite jealousy, induce envy.

Rare enough to set her apart as unapproachable because she'd held herself so to survive.

It's time to come to grips with where you came from, Heidi. It's long past time.

"Batter up!"

"Heidi!" Julie called. "That's you!"

Heidi swallowed hard, shook off the truth of what she'd soon have to deal with and took the bat from the other woman's hand.

"Go get 'em, girlfriend," Julie urged and Heidi answered, "They won't even know what hit 'em."

The bigger the words, the harder the fall.

She made her way across the infield's loose dirt, twisting the wooden bat handle between both palms, concentrating hard as she tried to remember if she'd walked away from a single "at bat" in her life with a hit.

The minute she stepped into the batter's box, she knew it wasn't going to happen. Not this time. Not with this center fielder, this pitcher and certainly not with this catcher crouched level with her, uh, right hip.

And poor Randy. The way this looked he'd end up stranded on first for the rest of his life. Heidi dug in with both feet, settled into her stance and narrowed her eyes toward Jack. Probably not a smart look because Jack, preparing his windup, leaned forward and returned the glare.

Only he couldn't keep a straight face. It started with a chuckle he hid behind his fist, grew into a laugh he buried in his glove, ended as a guffaw that had him doubled over while Heidi backed out of the box, propped a hand at her hip and scowled. *Oh, now he decides to have fun!*

"Sorry. I'm sorry." Jack put up one hand, put on an expression of complete seriousness and tried again. He did a good job, too, making it through the entire windup and delivery with no sign of his former descent into levity.

That was when Ben took over. "Hey, batte-batte-batte-batter. Batte-batte-batte-batter. SWING!"

Heidi swung. And missed. Not surprising in the least since she hadn't even seen the ball. She looked over Ben's head at Ronnie, the officiating father-to-be. "Can he do that?"

Ronnie wiped his sweaty forehead in the crook of his elbow. "Yes, ma'am. He can."

"Hmpf." She raised a high brow down at Ben. "I won't fall for it again."

"We'll see," he said and grinned roguishly, the dark hair and dark sunglasses and dark blue bandanna the uniform of the dread Pirate Tannen.

Damn distracting man. Damn distracting scar. She whipped her head up and away and dared Jack to bring it on. He did, she swung and missed. She knew she missed.

She didn't need the groans from the dugout or Randy's, "Eye on the ball, Heidi. Watch the ball," or Quentin's sympathetic shrug from the outfield or Jack's unsympathetic gloat.

And more than anything she certainly didn't need the low sexy chuckle behind her, way too close to her hip, close enough that she wasn't sure she didn't imagine the heat of Ben's body or the clean sweaty smell of his wet hair and skin.

She knew she didn't imagine her body's response, the shaking knees and sweating schoolgirl palms. Or the all grown-up flutter deep in her belly. Or the quiet insistent trembling closer to her heart.

Then Ben cleared his throat and said quietly, "You

know, Heidi. It's been fifteen years. Now that we've made it out of the parking lot, don't you think it's time we stopped trying to bust each other's balls?"

Thwack. Jack's third strike caught Heidi out and looking, but looking at the bane of her existence, not the pitch. She towered over and glowered down. "What I think is that if we're going to continue reliving our past, you should stand up and I'll see if I can finish knocking some sense into your hard head."

Ben stood slowly, pushing up on those well-toned legs until he ruled one side of the plate and Heidi ruled the other. The pulse in his neck matched the beat of her heart. The set of his shoulders was rigid, the set of his features was tight. Then the tic in his jaw slowly eased. And he smiled.

He tucked both ball and glove beneath one arm and pulled his shades from his face with the opposite hand. His eyes twinkled and his mouth twitched so Heidi never felt a hint of a threat when he waggled his fingers in a bold "come hither."

"You want me, baby? You come get me."

The tension on the field of the ballpark rose along with the heat in the air. Heidi could barely breathe, even though she pulled in one long breath after another. She considered flight, considered retreat, considered digging a hole to the center of the earth.

But this challenge was a part of their "long time coming" and she took an equally bold step forward.

She jabbed the head of the bat into Ben's six-pack abs and gave a gentle push. He stumbled backward theatrically, arms flailing wildly as he went down and dropped ball and glove and shades to the ground.

Heidi rolled her eyes. "If you're going to be this easy on me, I'm not going to waste the effort."

Ben grinned his cocky pirate grin and got to his feet. He reached forward and flicked the end of her nose. "You won't believe how incredibly easy I am."

"How incredibly arrogant, you mean," she said and this time jabbed a little harder.

He took another long slow-motion fall and landed flat on his backside, sending smoky dust rising in a cloud. A very effective pratfall judging by the gasps of the onlookers.

Struggling to his feet, he swiped the dirt from his rear and backed a step away. Heidi advanced, wielding her bat and giving the audience what they wanted to see. This was Mighty Heidi in her element, arguing her case, proving her point, defending The Joker's life.

Ben hit the chain-link backstop, feigned panic, crossed his arms over his face to ward off her imaginary blows. From the dugouts, the field and the bleachers, giggles and heckles and howls reached her ears, but Heidi didn't stop.

She pressed forward, adrenaline making good on the part of her attack not covered by the thrill of payback. When was the last time she'd felt this fire for anything but a case? *Oh, Ben. You're in for it now.*

She'd gone as far as she could go without pushing Ben through the backstop. Holding the broad head of the bat to his middle, she smiled sweetly and tapped the wood to his belly. "Now, watch my mouth and say, 'I'm sorry for distracting you, Heidi. I'm sorry I caused you to strike out.'"

Ben was silent for a moment, his gaze fastened on

her lips as instructed. Then his eyes flared and grew a smoky dusky green. "Do I?"

"Do you what?"

"Do I distract you, Heidi?"

"You know you did with all that batter chatter. Telling me to swing." She raised the bat, slowly touched the smooth tip to his chin.

And then her stomach clenched. She felt that she was quite out of breath. But still she slid the head of the bat along the length of his scar. The sound of her own voice barely reached her ears. "What did you think you were doing, Ben? Telling me to swing?"

"I meant at the ball, baby. Not at me." He took the bat from her hand and lowered it to the ground.

She blinked, frowned. *What just happened?* And why had he called her baby? And what was she doing standing so close when she'd seen last night that distance was vital?

Her eyes were level with his collarbone. His skin was damp and dusty. And since she was already out of her mind, she reached up and cleared a finger-wide path through the coating of grime.

His skin was resilient. Supple and healthy and glowing and hot. The hair on his chest deserved exploration. She softly raked three fingers through, stopping when Ben sucked in a sharp breath.

"What're you doin' here, Heidi? You gonna hit me? Hurt me? Tie me in knots and make me beg?" He smiled then. An evil smile. A twisted deviant devilish smile. "Or are you wanting to give these fine people the show they've been waiting to see for at least fifteen years?"

7

BEN TANNER HAD picked the wrong woman to mess
with. Because Heidi was in a serious don't-mess-
with-me mood. She'd struck out and let her team-
mates down, a minor offense. She'd threatened to
smack Ben again, although teasingly.

She was acting the jackass in front of people who
for years had expected nothing better from her—and
when she'd been so determined they'd walk away
from this weekend having changed their minds.

But more than any of those don't-mess-with-me
reasons causing smoke to pour from her ears was that
she was standing here with out-and-out lust on her
mind.

And that made her angry—at herself, at Ben, at the
way hormones and old times couldn't keep their
hands off one another.

It wasn't a nice lust, either. It was a lust with bedroom potential. A lust begging her to explore. This
man. His body. His body with hers. She couldn't believe that sex was what this weekend was coming
down to. Not when she'd arrived in Sherwood Grove
with purely adult goals and motives.

What? Like sex doesn't fit that category?

She was so out of her mind. If only Georgia could
see her now. No, she needed to keep Georgia out of

this. The other woman would only cheer Heidi on, then gloat with a big bad *I-told-you-so*.

Besides. It was time. They'd reached the midpoint of the weekend. And Ben *was* the reason she was here. She pulled in a deep breath, blew it out in a slow long stream.

And then she said, "You got my IOU on you, Ace?"

Ben took a minute to react, and his reaction was all Heidi had expected. He took her by the shoulders, his fingers slipping beneath the rayon fabric of her sleeveless white blouse, and then he was the aggressor, spinning her up against the backstop fence.

"I can have it on me—" he glanced at his dusty watch face "—in an hour. No, forget that. Come home with me. We can be there in thirty minutes."

What thrilled her most was that he was serious. Urgently serious. What made her stomach burn was that he was serious. Deadly serious.

Oh, he was serious. And she was going to be sick. He wanted her, this man, this man who had been an intrinsic part of her life since she was fifteen years old, wanted her.

And she wanted him. Here, on this ball field, in front of God and the opposing team. She wanted to make love with Ben Tannen. His nostrils flared, his eyes blistered and Heidi was lost in the fog of his heat.

She wanted to bathe him, to wash the dirt and grime from his body, to touch his wet skin, to feel him in soapsuds, to smell all the male parts so clean and so luscious.

She wanted to undress him, to slowly peel away his bandanna and finger the texture of his hair, to flip open the buttons of his fly, to see how he looked in nothing but briefs, to see how he looked in nothing at all.

She wanted to listen to the sound of his breathing, the sound of his voice, the sound of his pleasure and his pleasure in her. She wanted him naked. She wanted him inside of her. She wanted all those things and she wanted them now.

She'd wondered at times about women she'd represented, how they could get themselves into so much trouble based on hormone-driven choices.

Now, she understood.

She laughed, nervously, a sound that couldn't belong to her, Heidi Malone. "What's your hurry, Ace?"

"You're right." He lifted one—only one—exasperated hand from her shoulder, shoved the bandanna from his head and stuffed it into his pocket. "Right. What's the hurry. It's not like I've been waiting fifteen friggin' years."

"You have?" she said, her voice ingenuously soft. "You've been waiting for me?"

"Call it a sick and twisted fantasy, but yeah." He reached for a sprig of hair that had escaped the clasp of her ball cap and twirled it around his finger. "I've been waiting for you."

"I'm your fantasy?" She reached up and touched his face, and the hair that had fallen loose on his brow. "I don't think I've been anyone's fantasy before."

Ben's eyes slowly closed, slowly opened. His mouth pulled into a regretful smile. "You were everyone's fantasy, Heidi. Didn't you know that?"

"What do you mean?" she asked, and frowned at his statement. This was becoming ludicrous. What was it she'd been so blind to all these years?

"Nothing. Later." His annoyance was plain.

Her mood had shifted, taking on a hint of perturbation. They weren't even in a relationship and she already had a headache. Not a good sign.

"We can't go anywhere. We're in the middle of a ball game," she said, though most of the audience had long since dispersed.

"This ball game stopped about seven minutes ago." The hand still on her shoulder fondled the strap of her bra. "What we're in the middle of is a game with different rules."

"Rules?" Finally. The return of her backbone. "And who sets these rules?"

"I do. You do. We do."

"I see. And if I decide I don't want to play the game?"

"That's not going to happen," he said and reached for her hands.

He laced their fingers together and raised their joined hands. Hooking his fingers through the backstop fence, he gently held her there. His body wasn't quite as gentle when it pressed forward.

"You want to play just as much as I do. I can see it in your eyes."

She frowned, squinted. "No you can't."

He nodded, his lips fighting a twitch. "And I can see it in the way you're breathing."

That she didn't doubt for a minute. There was probably no one in the park who couldn't see the rise and fall of her chest, even with a sports bra mashing her breasts into pancakes.

"You have a wild imagination, Ben."

"It's in the way you hold your mouth, Heidi."

She released her tongue, which was caught between the bare edges of her teeth.

"And the way you let me so close. I don't think you've allowed this with many men, have you?"

She wasn't going to tell him. She wasn't going to tell him. She wasn't going to tell him, so she didn't say a word.

"I didn't think so," he answered, and then his mouth came down on hers.

It wasn't a very nice kiss. It was all body and all mouth, the kiss Heidi would have imagined had she any idea a man could kiss like this.

There was desperation and there was hunger and there was loneliness and relief. She knew all these things, could name every one, because Ben drew the same from her.

He drew more, as well. From the woman's deep, center of her body, he pulled up longing and rapture, which was the only word to describe the bliss she found in his mouth. Greed, which surprised her. She hadn't known she could want this badly.

And that it would be Ben she wanted...

Heidi squeezed his hand, leaned her head forward and gave him his answer, told him with her movements that he'd been right about all of it.

His tongue was so sweet as it slid against hers. Sweet and inviting and arousing and hot. His lips pressed hard, his beard scraped. His day off and he hadn't shaved. She liked that. She wanted to touch his face.

But he refused to let go of her hands. He held her fast when she made a weak struggle, growled a deep, "Uh-uh," in his throat. And the fight between her heart and her head lost the battle to her body.

She surrendered, giving in to Ben and sensation. His body was heated and hard and he smelled like the sun and clean sweat. His lips pulled at hers and his tongue tangled with hers and she pulled and tangled and kissed him right back.

Ben was the first to break contact. He opened his eyes and looked down, moving their joined hands to his hips, working to catch his own breath.

Her breath was long beyond catching. Her thumbs grazed the skin above his waistband and she sighed, then hooked them inside the denim. And inside the elastic of his shorts.

He hissed in a breath. "What're you doing to me, Heidi?"

She lifted her chin, met his eyes. "Playing this new game you started. Using my rules."

"I think I like your rules." He smiled, let go of her hands then, and moved *his* fingers to *her* waist, *his* thumbs to *her* waistband and beneath.

She whimpered softly; she couldn't help it, and she hoped he couldn't hear. But from the start of this contact he'd heard her every silent entreaty. So, of course he heard the one which reached his ears.

"Heidi. I want to touch you."

"You are touching me."

"No," he said and moved his fingers. "I want to *touch* you."

She answered him with her hands, sliding the flat of her palms from his waist to his ribs. It was all she could say.

Ben went on, his words barely reaching her ears. "I want you to touch me."

"I am touching you."

"No." He shook his head, resting his forehead on hers. His voice was tight when he said again, yet for the first time, "I want you to *touch* me."

She wanted to touch him. The way he asked. The way he begged. The way he wanted. How could she not want to please this man? He'd been everything to her all those years ago and her heart had not forgotten. It beat with his pulse even now.

But her mind remembered and she sighed, backing that first difficult step away from the moment. It was then that her common sense had room to intrude, her logic the space to prevail. He may have been everything to her then, but he could be nothing to her now—not until she'd repaired the ancient damage.

For even more than she owed that to Ben, she owed it to herself.

A loud intrusive cough drew Heidi's attention. She blinked slowly, accepting what her peripheral vision had insisted was the truth. They had an audience. A captive audience. A captive audience of three.

At her groan, Ben cut his eyes to the left, to the right, then he reached for Heidi's hands where they remained measuring the width of his ribcage.

He slid his palms from her wrists up her bare arms to her shoulders and, holding her captive like a pirate's possession, he swooped down and plundered her mouth one last time.

Then he stepped back, looked at Randy on his right, Jack on his left and shrugged. Arms crossed, the two men nodded at one another and moved in. Taking hold of Ben's upper biceps, they dragged him away. His heels left twin tracks in the dirt.

Heidi rolled her eyes and leaned into Quentin's side as he walked up and wrapped an arm around her shoulder. "Now that was worth the price of the trip."

He had no idea. "Glad you feel like you got your money's worth."

I know I did.

THE SHERWOOD GROVE Country Club had been built during the years Heidi had been absent from the Austin area. The impressive white stone facade stood as a testimony to wealth, guarding a section of the city into which she'd never had entrance as a child.

Amused by the valet's wide-eyed reaction to her sleek sports car, she slipped the claim check into her red evening bag and made her way up the flagstone walkway winding between pink-and-white roses and accents of deep summer green.

Smiling at the doorman, she took a deep breath and, full steam ahead, slipped inside as he held open the door. Funny how she felt completely at ease in the grand foyer of plush pink, gold and white, even while a tiny voice inside her head insisted she didn't belong.

She did belong. She fit in and had as much right to be here as any Tannen. Her designer dress of scarlet silk fell in classic lines from the capped sleeves on her shoulders to the floor. The neckline plunged discreetly, but daringly. The look fairly oozed Hollywood glamour.

Her shoes were Chanel. Her one accessory, a jeweled cuff bracelet, was elegantly understated. Her hair was swept up in a sleek chignon. She dared anyone to find evidence of the river kid who, unwelcome and unwanted, had spent four years at Johnson High.

Yet that's exactly who she was beneath the dress and the shoes and the bracelet that together cost half as much as she'd earned her first year out of law school. Almost as much, in fact, as the debt she'd repaid Ben Tannen.

The first debt, she amended. The monetary debt. She still had another debt to repay.

And she would. Before the end of the night she'd insist they talk about the assault. Because they couldn't take the night anywhere else, couldn't take this afternoon's game to its natural conclusion, until they did.

The ballroom beckoned, the orchestra playing a song from the big band era that had Heidi's fingers running keys on an imaginary sax. God, it had been so long since she'd played.

She missed it in a melancholy, regretful sort of way. The way one might miss childhood innocence. Because when she'd sold herself to Ben those fifteen years ago, she'd lost more than her self-respect.

She'd lost everything good in her life, all she'd held dear since her father had died. She'd lost the pride that had kept her from falling into her mother's gutter, and the decency she'd used to keep herself separate from the river kid life she'd survived.

But most of all she'd lost the belief that respect and

pride and decency mattered to those who'd once judged her on where she came from. Her values had meant nothing when she didn't have a portfolio or a pedigree.

She'd lived with what her classmates, their parents, her teachers thought of her during those years. But she couldn't live with what she'd thought of herself. Because, in the end, she'd taken a man's money. She'd been desperate, and allowed a man to buy her dignity—a sin worse than the added indignity of promising her body.

Ben hadn't known what he'd done, and he couldn't be faulted. He'd behaved the way everyone who lived in his world did. And she'd behaved the same. She wondered if the contact he'd made in college had been an attempt to collect, wondered if that was all he wanted now.

Well, she'd find out soon enough, wouldn't she, she thought, and stepped into the middle of the music.

The first couple she spotted was Randy and Julie. They stood inside the ballroom's wide double doors talking to Ronnie and Starr. It occurred to Heidi that Randy was the one member of The Deck she hadn't spent much time alone with this weekend.

He was also the one who'd been telling tales to Julie. Which made him a good candidate for Heidi's first mission of the night—to get to the bottom of all this talk about the feelings she'd stirred, the whispers that had gone on behind her back both this weekend and in high school.

She walked up to the foursome, wiggled her fingers in a friendly hello to the pregnant couple, winked at Julie with a shared female understanding and pulled Randy away with the crook of one finger. He didn't even hesitate, but followed like she was the Pied Piper and he was a rat.

"This song made me think of you," the lovable rat himself said, once they'd reached the dance floor.

He took her hand, placed his other at her waist and guided her easily through the crowd. "You remember that first day you showed up in the practice room? That song you played? This reminds me of that."

"It does, doesn't it?" Heidi said then fell silent, hoping the less she said the more Randy would say, increasing her chances for solving this mystery about what everyone thought about her.

"I had no idea what it was you were playing," Randy said. "I don't think the other guys did, either, but it didn't matter. All that mattered was that you got it right. Every note was dead-on."

She nodded her acknowledgment of the compliment. "I learned from my dad, who learned from his dad—"

"And so on and so on and so on?"

She laughed. "Something like that. I'd played since I was able to hold his sax. Before that even, really. My dad had this chair." She hadn't thought about that chair in years. "Big and cushy and brown. He'd sit on the edge of the cushion. And I'd stand between his knees while he held the horn and showed me how to key. I couldn't have been more than five or six."

"I always wondered who taught you to play. You played like you'd been taking private lessons for years. But I assumed that, well, that—"

"That coming from the river I could hardly afford private lessons?" she asked and raised a brow.

His face reddened and he took a misstep. "Sorry. I need to be more careful where I put my feet."

"It's okay. You missed all but one toe."

He chuckled, deftly guided her out of the mainstream of the dance floor. "No. I meant I need to stop sticking them into my mouth."

"Oh. That." She slid the hand holding her evening bag higher on his shoulder, looked him in the eye and smiled. "Well, your assumption wasn't too far off the mark. I couldn't have afforded to pay for private lessons."

"But you didn't have to. You had your dad."

"Until I was eight. After that, I only had myself and a lot of practice."

"Well, yourself did a damn good job with all that practice." He spun her away, twirled her back. "You amazed more than a few people, you know."

Ah-ha. The exact direction she'd hoped to take this conversation. "No. I didn't know."

"I didn't think you did," he said and then he didn't say any more, dang it. He just led her into another dance as the orchestra played on.

So much for *ah-ha.* It was time to pull out Mighty Heidi's arsenal for dealing with a reluctant witness. "Julie mentioned that you said that to her. That you didn't think I knew a lot of what was said about me." Pause and step and pause and, "She also told me that there wasn't a single member of The Deck who thought of me as one of the guys."

This time Randy's misstep caused Heidi to misstep

and knocked them both into Ben...who was dancing with Maryann Stafford.

"Hey, Ben. Maryann." Randy nodded toward the other couple. "Thanks for the save."

"What're friends for?" Ben asked, his eyes fast devouring Heidi's face, her eyes, her neckline, her mouth.

She could hardly remember where to put her feet, poor Randy, what with the fire in Ben's eyes. She was drifting, she was dreaming, she was dancing. She was in Ben's arms, on his bed, beneath his body...

Until Maryann broke the spell. "Randy, sweetie. I am so glad I was able to get away tonight. I haven't had a chance this weekend to see much of you at all."

Randy's mouth twisted wryly. "Well, now, Maryann. There's not really a lot I want you to see."

Heidi turned her head to hide her giggle, then glanced back and caught the get-me-the-hell-out-of-here roll of Ben's eyes. His jacket and tie were a severe black, his shirt a stark starched white.

The roguish pirate again, she thought. Getting stuck with Maryann tonight served him right for throwing all those pool parties in high school.

Maryann's low-throated chuckle was perfectly timed, and perfectly nauseating. "You haven't changed a bit, Randy. You're still the cut-up king." She reached in front of Heidi to lay a possessive hand along Randy's cheek. "I always said you should've been The Joker."

"But, then, what would we have done with Heidi?" Randy asked, looking exaggeratedly confused by the woman's suggestion. Between Ben-about-to-walk-the-plank and Randy-to-the-rescue,

Heidi was having a hard time keeping a straight face. These four men of hers were just too much.

Maryann frowned, as if searching the unused banks of her memory. "Oh, yes. Heidi. Whatever happened to the poor little thing?"

"The poor little thing?" Ben and Randy chimed in unison, then Randy added, "You mean the girl who held The Deck together? Who was responsible for more than half the damn ensemble trophies in Johnson High's case?"

"Was she really? I had no idea." Maryann pressed tighter to Ben.

Probably making sure he noticed what she'd bought to hang the top of this season's two-piece on, Heidi thought, wincing at the new low she'd reached.

She smiled, at Ben first, then at Maryann's profile, so it didn't matter that her expression wasn't convincingly kind. "Yes. I was. Really."

Maryann whipped her head Heidi's direction. "You?"

"Yep. Poor little me." Heidi wiggled her fingers at the other woman just as Randy spun away, leaving the dread pirate Tannen to deal with Maryann and her cleavage, which gaped almost as widely as her mouth.

Randy whirled Heidi completely off the dance floor then, to a cozy table near the front wall of floor-to-ceiling windows overlooking the Sherwood Grove golf course.

"You want a drink?" he asked, signaling a passing server and grabbing two flutes of champagne from the tray. He handed one to Heidi, then smoothed out the white linen tablecloth. "Some shindig, huh?"

"The rich get richer." Hadn't she once said that to Ben? Heidi searched out the dancing couple, found them weaving through the crowd near the center of the room, found Maryann trying hard to crack Ben's stone face. *As if you're woman enough, sister.*

"He's not going far."

At Randy's declaration, Heidi returned her attention to the table and away from the ballroom floor. "I was just making sure Maryann's top hadn't fallen off."

Randy cast a glance over Heidi's shoulder, shook his head. "It's not going to fall anywhere. Not with those...hangers."

"I'm not sure. Ben's laser vision might dissolve the silicone. He looks to be on the verge of a meltdown." Actually, he looked like an advertisement for heartburn."

"Trust me." Randy pulled her attention away from the dance floor. "He's not the least bit interested in Maryann, though I'm sure the opposite is true. She's available again, and on the prowl."

"Available. Is that anything like open for business?"

"Me-ow." Randy added a hiss. "What it means is that she's aggravating. Like junk mail. No. If Ben does a meltdown, it'll be over your red dress."

"You know, Randy...sweetie—" she added the latter with Maryann's sugared inflection "—I've heard so many innuendoes and insinuations this weekend that I'm immune. There is not a thing you can say that will get a rise out of me."

"Ben loves you."

Heidi's heart stopped, started again. *Breathe, Heidi.*

Breathe. Dizzy, she sucked in a sharp breath, and looked through the purple haze of unconsciousness at the calculated winner's smile on Randy's face.

The rat! He'd said Ben loved her. Not that Ben was in love with her. She was going to kill him. Strangle him. Bury him in that very expression. But, before she could work out the goriest of details, Randy spoke.

"The thing is," he said, his voice low. "We all love you."

Heidi blinked. "What?"

"You know what I said about remembering that first day you walked into the practice room?" She nodded and he went on. "Well, there's a reason I remember it so well. The same reason Jack and Quentin and Ben won't forget it, either.

"This is going to sound as corny as hell, but we all lost our hearts that day." He rubbed a hand over his forehead. "You walked in looking like you'd dressed at a garage sale on the way to school, acting like you were in charge of the whole damn band no matter how bad your haircut was.

"But then you played that sax. You got off on that song like you were Duke Ellington or someone."

Heidi smiled through misty eyes. "He played trumpet. Not sax."

"I know. I'm the trumpet guy, remember?" He cocked his chair back, lifted an imaginary horn. "But you get my drift. You were magic. And you cast some kind of spell that day that we all took four years' worth of ribbing over."

"You got ribbed?" Her heart pounded wildly, her eyes watered. "Because of me?"

"Yeah. Because of you." He leaned forward and,

taking her hand in his, he squeezed. "You were talented and gutsy. A survivor. You didn't care what everyone thought about you, about what you wore, about how you got to school every day, about the house you went home to at night. The rest of us didn't care about anything else."

He was so wrong about that. So very, very wrong. She'd cared. She'd just never thought anyone else had.

"You intimidated the hell out of the other kids because you didn't put up with the bullshit. From anyone." He shifted nervously, released her hand to rake his fingers through his hair. "Hell, you know what kind of grades I made. And you know I hated being smart. But you wouldn't let me blow it all off."

How could he do this to her? Here? Now? After all these years? Lifting her drink with unsteady fingers, she turned her gaze toward the window where the golf course rolled away into the dark. She couldn't even see the first green because of the tears in her eyes.

Why had he waited so long to tell her what she'd needed to know? That she'd mattered. That she'd made a difference. Why did it feel like her heart was being ripped from her chest to know that she had had an impact? That she hadn't been an outcast. That she hadn't been alone.

Oh, God. She hadn't been alone. She sniffed, looked back and smiled. Her voice shook when she said, "For being smart, you were really stupid."

"Yeah. I was." Finally he relaxed and reached out a finger to lift an unshed tear from her lashes. "I'm not saying you made me see it then. In fact, I didn't see it until a long time later."

"Then why did you listen?"

"Because it was a lot easier to do what you said than to have to listen to you if I didn't."

"Oh, well. Thanks. It's nice to know I could be depended on to make your life miserable."

"Miserable?" He shook his head. "No. Interesting? Yes. I never knew anyone so focused. Nothing distracted you. It was like you didn't have room in your life for concerts or parties or anything that didn't have to do with band. Or with your future."

"You're right. I didn't."

He shook his head, laughed. "I still don't know how you managed. But you did. And that had a big impact on me. It had a big impact on a lot of people."

She wasn't going to tell him how she managed. That was one secret that would stay with her and Ben. And now with Quentin. "Yeah. I can see how much impact it had on Maryann Stafford. 'Heidi, who?'"

"She knew who you were. Everyone here knows who you are. They just don't know what to say."

She didn't care. It didn't matter. How could it when she had the love of her four men? "They don't have to say anything, Randy. You just said it all."

His face pulled into a smug male grin as he looked up and over her shoulder. "No. Not all. There's more."

Uh-oh. "More?"

"More. And he's headed straight this way."

8

If he didn't get off the dance floor, get across the room to Randy's table, get Heidi to himself and soon, Ben was going to blow a gasket. His anticipation had started weeks ago, a pot set to a slow simmer on the flame of her RSVP.

He'd wondered for years if he'd ever see her again, if his curiosity would find satisfaction, if their unfinished business would come to a close. If he was the only one who felt they had a circle to complete.

She'd answered that question in the club, with the language of her body and the poetry of her kiss, starting a twenty-four-hour slow burn in his gut. He'd thought about antacid, then thought, why bother. He wouldn't take a watering can to a barn fire. Same thing.

On the ball field the heat had intensified. She'd been a fiery little thing this afternoon, both barrels of frustration blazing beautifully with an untamed heat. He knew what she was feeling, the male version anyway, and the added fuel of her passion had his flame turned on high.

Now, finally, here they were tonight. And his blood had reached full boil.

He'd been watching her since she'd arrived, in the foyer as she took in her surroundings, the guileless child impressed by the opulence, the worldly woman who'd seen it all before. She'd lived both sides of wealth's coin.

He'd watched her on the dance floor in Randy's arms, watched the tilt of her chin as she laughed, the life in her eyes, a sparkle he'd never seen until last night when she'd met his gaze in the club—when she'd refused to flinch at his reaction to seeing her again. Seeing all that she'd wanted him to see.

She was beautiful. He'd never doubted she would be once she grew beyond the need for the scarecrow hair, the flea-market fashion, the armor of the anger and the attitude. But the truth beat the pants off his fantasy.

That hair he'd so hated yet had fit her so well had grown into a cascade of curls he wanted draped on his skin. His fingers knew the texture, but his fingers didn't count. He wanted to feel the slide of that silk across his chest, across his abdomen, and lower.

He wanted to feel her mouth there as well. That mouth that had always been so sassy. That mouth that he'd now kissed twice and would be kissing thoroughly again before the hour was out.

She'd never worn makeup. She wore it artfully now. And, yeah, so sue him, it added to his fantasy.

He liked looking at the color on her skin, at the hair she managed to hold up with one tiny clip. He liked the fit of her clothes, tight in places, concealing in others, because both alluded to what lay beneath.

But more than all of that, he couldn't wait to see her with her skin scrubbed clean after kisses and sleep, her hair tumbled and tangled from his hands, her clothing tossed alongside his on the bedroom floor and her skin bare.

That's how he wanted Heidi. That's how he planned to have her, and soon. That is, if he made it through the crowd milling around the edge of the dance floor and over to the damn table she shared with Randy.

He knew she saw him coming. She was looking back over her shoulder, her knuckles white against a glass of pink champagne. Her eyes widened with each step he took closer, the set of her mouth grew less certain.

He'd been trying to get to her all night. It was taking way too long. She was wearing red. And revealing a lot of skin he'd never seen before and wanted to see closer, wanted to touch, wanted to taste.

Then, finally, he was there and she was sitting only two feet away, but his throat was tight and his tongue was tied and the present had tangled up in the tails of the past.

All he could think to do was hold out his hand. "Let's go."

Unsure, she looked up. "Let's go?"

"Let's go," he repeated.

Glancing at Randy, she reached for her bag, drew it slowly across the table. Randy shrugged, nodded with enthusiasm, shooed her away with a resounding, "Let's go!"

She got to her feet, placed her fingers in Ben's, met his gaze with a no-guts-no-glory expression. "Let's go."

It was about damn time.

Enclosing her slender fingers in his, Ben headed for

the closest exit. The set of glass doors opened onto a flagstone terrace landscaped in the same pink roses lining the club's front walkway.

The music spilled into the balmy June night, bringing with it couples who'd escaped the press of ballroom bodies to dance quietly, privately, to sit on scattered terrace benches and talk, kiss, share a drink, touch.

Ben didn't even stop. He twined his fingers through Heidi's, pulled her down the terrace steps and out onto the lawn's winding trails.

He wanted privacy. Total privacy. No subdued laughter, no intimate whispers, no *it's been a long time* intrusions. He was running out of patience as it was.

"Ben, wait!"

Heidi tugged at his hand and he slowed, barely, looking right and left. Dammit. Nothing. No place offered the seclusion he sought.

There were too many people, too many wide-open spaces. A golf course, a few trees. No secluded benches. Or beds.

Who was he kidding?

His urgency wasn't going to wait for a bed. What he felt for this woman had been building for fifteen years. Fifteen years he'd lived with the fantasy. And here she was. Real. Flesh and blood. The woman he wanted.

"Ben, wait!"

This time she jerked her hand free of his hold. He stopped because he had to, turned and stared. What the hell was he doing?

Her chest rose and fell with the exertion of their flight. Her eyes shone wildly in the light of the moon.

Spirals of hair escaped their clasp and twirled like tempting ribbons on her skin.

She was flushed and fevered and he stirred at the sight of her. One purposeful step at a time, she walked toward him. Her smile, as it spread across her face, stirred him more. Her hand came up, she placed it along his jaw, tracing the line of his scar, and he stirred completely.

"I'm not going to run out on you, Ben." The stroke of her finger was erotically soft, the stroke of her breathy voice arousing. "I'm not going to run. Ever. Again."

He had her. She was his. Her eyes, the eyes which even his dreams looked into, told him that truth. He breathed deeply. The tight knot that had seized his gut released its fire. Liquid heat spread through his body and his knees shook.

He wanted to bring her pleasure. More than taking his fill of this woman, he wanted to make her burn— *for* him, *with* him, all over him. Hands on his hips, he watched her smile grow wise and knowing.

And this time when he stirred he knew he was in trouble. Emotional trouble. Trouble that began with a capital *H* and had held him captive for years.

He blew out a long telling breath. Later. He'd deal with that later. Right now he had a more pressing problem to resolve. He wrapped his fingers around her wrist more gently this time. "Come on, Heidi."

"Come on where?"

He searched the grounds madly, the tennis courts, the golf course, the pool... "This way."

She came willingly which, even after her words of

reassurance, came as a relief. He was so close to having her that not having her wasn't an option.

He'd wanted her in high school, but then he'd been seventeen and horny. That was a lust that had confused him, tangled up as it was with his feelings of friendship.

He'd wanted her the years after the assault and the note. That want was tied up in anger and revenge. Sicker, yes, but much easier to understand.

He wanted her now because she was Heidi who was strong and sassy. Who answered his catcalls with a baseball bat and had the class, the grace, the feminine allure that couldn't be surgically implanted or donned with designer labels, that made a man stand up and take notice.

"Where are we going?" she asked, breathless behind him.

He smiled his first smile of the evening, felt the first easing of nerves. Oh, this was going to be good. "I have an urge."

"An urge? You do?"

Nodding, he kept his pace steady though his legs screamed to run. "Actually, I've had it for years."

"Have you seen a doctor about this?"

He laughed. Good? Ha! This was going to be great. "No need. The cure is right in front of my face."

They'd reached the gate that led into the fenced-off pool enclosure. The area had been locked up for the reunion night festivities, but Ben punched the code into the electronic keypad and guided Heidi through.

Security lamps glowed yellow from the enclosure's four corners, lighting the walkway from the gate to the pool house and on to the water's edge.

She waited for him to secure the lock then said, "Isn't this area off-limits?"

"Membership does have its privileges." It also had its rules, a dozen or so of which he was breaking. *So sue me*, he thought.

"What are we doing here?" she whispered, though there was no one around to hear. Or to see.

Which fit in perfectly with Ben's plans. He looked down at her, feeling the tide of desire rise. "You always said no when I asked you to my pool parties. This time I'm going to make you come."

Her eyes glittered beneath the brilliance of the moon and a light even brighter that came from within. "You are?"

Wrapping one arm around her waist, he pulled her to him. "Yes. Several times."

"How many is several?"

It was going to be one less if she didn't stop looking at him that way. "How many do you want it to be?"

"How much time do we have?"

"Less than we did two minutes ago." And once again he took her hand.

They made their way to the pool house where Ben pulled open the door to the breezeway. Bypassing the workout room and the sauna, the locker rooms and showers, he grabbed a stack of towels from those freshly folded and pushed back into the open air with the smell of chlorine and the night.

Heidi's heels clicked against the pool decking as she followed him to the water's edge. He grabbed a chaise lounge, dragged it behind him, shrugged off his suit jacket once he'd stopped.

"Ben?" Heidi faced him from the other side of the

chair. Her voice was steady, but her face showed signs of hesitation. "What're you doing?"

He pulled at the knot of his tie, draped it over his jacket where it lay across the back of the chair. "Going to a pool party. With you."

Tentatively, she placed her evening bag on the foot of the lounger, uncuffed her bracelet and tucked it inside. "Should we be here? Is it safe?"

"We're safe. The pool house blocks the view from the gate. No one can get in without the code. And only one or two of our ex-classmates are members anyway."

He worked his buttons through their holes and tossed his shirt to the chair. Then he toe-heeled off his shoes, pulled off his socks, his watch and reached for his belt.

"Ben?" Heidi hadn't moved, but stood watching him undress, stood staring at his half-naked body with the moon and the stars and intensity in her eyes. "I don't have a swimsuit."

"You have a bra and panties?"

Nodding, she closed her eyes, pulled in a breath, blew it out through pursed lips and looked up. Then kicked off her shoes and smiled.

It was a wicked smile. An evil smile. The smile of a temptress wearing red. He ground his jaw and suppressed the erection he had rising.

He needed patience. He needed control. He didn't need to frighten her before he'd convinced her to follow his lead.

He opened his fly and waited.

Heidi lifted one shoeless foot to the seat of the chair, raised her skirt and reached for the band of her thigh-high stockings. Ben groaned. Heidi's legs in sheer thigh-high stockings.

Breathe, Ben. Breathe. Imaginary fingers drummed against his heart. Silently he watched as she took her time, drew her fingers higher, slipped them beneath the lace-banded tops, eased down the white nylon and pulled the fluff free from toes with nails of bright red.

She repeated the process, giving him a nice long look at her other leg—a look he took. He saw her smooth skin, the curve of her calf, her strong shapely thigh, and then he saw a flash of white panty. Groaning again, he moved his gaze away, to the dip of her neckline.

Breathe, Ben. Breathe. Her breasts swayed as she worked off the second stocking and he gave up fighting his body. Her stockings now lay on his jacket and shirt and the sight had him wanting a drink to wet his mouth. And then she reached for the zipper on the back of her dress.

He watched as her bare arms lifted to release the first few inches of the closure, then lowered to reach behind her back and finish the job. The motion pulled her dress tight over the breasts he was so close to having.

He didn't care if he ever breathed again.

And then she stopped, met his gaze, arched a brow and said, "Well?"

"Well what?" What was she doing talking? Why had she stopped?

"It's your turn."

"My turn?"

She nodded, took two steps toward him. "Our feet

are both bare. Our zippers are down. We're even. The next move is yours."

Ah. But she was so wrong. He shook his head. "We're not even."

"How so?"

"You're still wearing your top," he said and felt his nostrils flare, felt sweat break out across his bare chest, felt a full throb of his erection against the elastic of his shorts.

He wanted to see her strip, not necessarily to see her naked. He wanted to be closer, eye to eye, mouth to mouth, skin to skin when she finally bared all.

And he wanted to do the baring.

He wanted to release the clasp of her bra, to pull the straps down her shoulders, to tease the cups across the nipples he'd dreamed about for years since that day in her attic, to hold her full flesh when her breasts were free.

Of course to be able to do any of that he'd have to be able to move. And right now he was rooted in place because the sleeves of her dress were coming down.

"Wait," he said and put up one hand.

She halted, questioned him with her eyes and waited. And waited, waited with her feet bare and her legs bare and her dress close to coming off. And while she waited, he tried to decide why he'd stopped her.

This moment had been so incredibly long in coming. And now that it was here he wanted everything to be perfect. He wanted it to last forever because never in his life had he felt anything so right.

Heidi had been his since that first day in the band

hall when she'd singled him out of the four. She was here with him now and he didn't want her to think this was a payback, a collection, a calling it even of any sorts.

This was about one man and one woman and the pleasure between.

"Ben? What's wrong?" she asked and frowned.

Nothing was wrong. This was all so right. Why was he even worried? He shook his head, blinked hard, lifted one corner of his mouth. "Just enjoying the view."

She took another step closer and another, lowered her dress one more inch and one more. Her eyes flashed fire when she asked, "Were you wanting a closer look?"

The look he wanted required Braille. He swallowed hard, shoved his hand in his pants pockets, and wrapped his right fist around the strip of foil packets he was so glad he'd decided to bring.

He shook his head because he couldn't speak, nodded for her to continue.

She did, shimmying out of the slip of red silk in one long full-body, hip-rolling shake. The pool of red swallowed her feet and she stood there in a bra and panties that would never pass for a swimsuit.

Good thing this party was private, that this was his show and his show alone.

She wore white scraps of nothing, sheer enough to see shadows and outlines and suggestions of all the things female so close to his reach. The cups of the bra were lace-edged and cut low, the legs of the panties lace-edged and cut high.

His hands itched to close over her bottom, to pull

her close, to grind his hips against her. To lose his pants before he did any of that.

"Ben? I think it's still your turn." She stepped out of the puddle of silk, reached down to pick up the dress and exposed a lot of pink-tipped skin in the process.

After draping the dress across his discarded shirt and jacket, she rounded the head of the chair, taking slow barefoot steps toward the pool's edge and presenting him with a full view of her back.

Dipping the toes of one foot in the water, she glanced back over her shoulder. "Ben?"

"Huh?" he grunted.

"I said it's your turn."

"My turn?" His turn for what? How could he think about anything when, but for two straps of elastic across her back, she was bare from nape to heel.

Tendrils of hair tickled her neck and his imagination. Her shoulders were beautifully rounded, her back beautifully strong. Her waist was narrow, her hips curvy, her bottom a fit to fill his hands. Her legs went on forever and he wanted them around his waist. Which meant he had to get naked.

He shucked his pants, tossed them carelessly to the chair. And missed. Who cared? He was finally down to his white briefs and wearing no more than Heidi.

Now they were even. Both standing at the pool's edge and fully filling out what underwear they wore.

Leaving two feet between them, he moved to stand at her right. She cut a glance his way, taking him in from top to bottom. Her eyes held curiosity, interest, appreciation. His head swelled, along with other parts of his anatomy.

And then while he was contemplating his state of painful bliss, Heidi jumped into the shallow end of the pool. The splash of water settled to lap at her breasts. Envious, Ben lowered his body and sat on the edge, dangling his legs over the cement lip and into the pool.

Heidi walked toward him, stopping when she reached his knees. He wanted her to come closer, to touch him, to step between his legs...

A droplet of water fell from her lashes, another from her nose. Her hair was still up and still dry. They stayed there, Heidi in the water, her bra now wet and transparent, and Ben sitting on the edge holding onto his last shred of control.

And then Heidi beckoned with a lazy blink of her eyes, the crook of one finger and a low-pitched request. "This isn't going to be much of a party if I'm the only one getting wet."

He growled, pushed off and launched into the water. Unlike Heidi, Ben felt the need for a complete dunking and when he came up for air she was waiting. He walked toward her slowly, the water tugging at his limbs. She backed away one step at a time until she came up against the pool wall.

"Looks like you won't be going any further," he said, though the entire Olympic-size pool stretched in front of her.

She waved her hands through the water, creating ripples all around. "Are you saying I've gone far enough?"

"I'm almost amazed you've gone this far."

Her chin came up, her hands stopped. "I told you I wasn't going to run out on you, Ben."

"I know. I heard you."

"I heard you, too."

"What did I say?"

"You invited me to your pool party. And you told me you were going to make me come."

"So I did," he said wanting to spread her legs and bury himself in her body, wanting first for her to ask him to.

"Well?"

"Well what?"

"I'm here. At your party." She reached out her arms along the pool edge, suspending her body while she kicked out with her legs. "When are you going to make me come?"

He was near enough now to touch her, so he reached out one hand and trailed one finger from the hollow of her throat over her breastbone and between her breasts, down her belly, through her navel to the edge of her panties.

He dipped his finger inside to find her flesh swollen and her nub hard. She gasped as he stroked her once, twice, circling the pad of his finger around her while she squirmed to work him inside.

It took the steel control of his sudden super powers to pull away. But he did. And then he closed his eyes and counted to ten to recover.

He was only up to three when Heidi spoke.

"Ben?"

He opened his eyes. "Yes?"

"Would you do that again?"

"All right." He ground out the two words.

"But this time don't stop."

"Okay." He groaned out the one.

"And this time I want more than your finger."

Like there was a man alive who could say no to that?

He stepped forward, boosted her onto the edge of the pool and finally, finally, finally buried his face between her breasts. Her skin was cool from the water, warm from her heat. He reached behind her to release the catch of her bra.

He didn't have a chance to see the flesh he'd bared because she took his head and guided his mouth to her breast. She was sweet and textured and gumdrop hard and he rolled her nipple with his tongue.

Her body arched. She leaned back on the palms she'd planted on the deck behind her. He couldn't get close enough, dammit. Kissing his way to her other breast, he placed his hands at her waist, lifted her from her perch, lowered her onto his body.

Her arms came up to wrap around his neck, his thigh came up to press between hers. He swept their bodies back into the water. Looking into her eyes, he swirled her to the center of the pool, moving his thigh and rubbing circles on the hot spot she ground against him.

"Oh, Ben," she said and lightly shuddered, raining kisses on his forehead, on his eyelids, on his cheeks. "Don't stop. Please don't stop."

He'd only gotten started. He never intended to stop. He held her naked bottom where she rode his thigh and leaned forward, exploring her mouth with his tongue while he busied his hands behind her.

Securing the strap of her thong in one hand, the band of elastic in the other, he yanked. Hard. Separating the seam and stripping her bare.

"Oh, Ben," she said as now only his shorts remained as a barrier between them, as her feminine flesh made full contact with his thigh. She scooted farther up his leg, closer to the part of him she sought.

And then she said, "It's your turn again."

He carried her back to the pool's edge, away from the underwater lights and into chest-deep water. Once there, once his body held hers in place, she moved her hands to his waist and the elastic of his shorts.

He hissed, struggled for control, knew he'd never find it in the dark, in the water, in Heidi's arms. Her hands were on his skin now, working the wet material over his hips, over his erection. Then she raised one leg and, with a foot between his thighs, took his shorts to his feet.

"Now we're even." She wrapped her legs around him, reaching between their bodies to take him in her hands for the first time.

Her hands and the water and her legs were too much. The waiting was over. He grabbed the leg of the trousers dragging the deck. With Heidi kissing his neck, running her hands over his chest and his back and his rump and his erection, he fumbled in the pocket.

Underwater condom application was not the easiest thing he'd ever done, and made even harder by his degree of hardness and the pressure of Heidi's great expectations and her roaming hands. But finally he was sheathed and ready.

He positioned himself where he felt her heat, placed her hands on his shoulders, his on the pool edge behind. Rocking forward with his body, he sought entry, pushing slowly upward and meeting resistance.

She was a virgin. His pulse pounded madly through his veins. He screeched to a stop. "Heidi?"

"You're beautiful, Ben. So hard. So smooth. So big." Her mouth moved to his, devoured his, her hands moved to his rump. She urged him on with her heels then gently nipped his lip. "And if you stop again, I'm going to kill you."

She was giving him her virginity and his heart had never been so full.

"Please, Ben? Hurry?" Her fingers dug into the backs of his thighs.

Impatient virgin wench. He still couldn't believe this was happening. Why was this gorgeously passionate woman a virgin? "I'm not going to hurry your first time, sweetheart.

"Hold onto the edge of the pool. Wrap your legs around my waist. That's it," he coaxed as she followed his instructions. He really liked a woman who followed his instructions.

And then it was time to get serious. He looked into her eyes and asked the question he had to ask, the answer to which might possibly kill him. "Heidi? Are you sure?"

She answered him with a low moaning kiss, tenderly using her tongue to stroke and beg him to take her. So he took her. Slowly. Entering her tight, oh, so tight, body.

She gasped into his mouth. He stopped and she whimpered, urging him forward with fingers and heels and very strong thighs.

"Heidi, baby. Wait." It was going to be all over with if she didn't. "I don't want to hurt you."

She held his face, kissed his eyelids, his cheekbone, the beginning of his scar before meeting his eyes. "The hurt can't be helped. But you'll make it all better. I know you will."

She was beautiful. Stunningly beautiful. Her eyes were trusting and honest, her smile giving and warm. And she was offering him what she'd never offered another man.

Why? Later. Later. Now was the time to take her slow and easy, to move only at her command, to soothe the pain she suffered, to see to her pleasure. His mouth descended to hers, his tongue seeking entrance with the same gentle force he applied beneath the water's surface.

His stroke deepened, the pressure from her body eased and he was fully enveloped. He stopped to find his control, stopped for Heidi to find comfort. But her eager cries gave him license to move. He increased the rhythm of his strokes, gritting his teeth at her insistence that he move faster, that he fill her deeper.

She was wild around him and the water splashed and her fingers dug into his skin as her spasms took hold. He swallowed her cries and poured his own into her mouth, following her down into ecstasy.

Long minutes later, normal breathing returned. Water cooled overheated skin until Heidi shivered. Ben pulled his body from hers and held her close to warm her. She shuddered again and gooseflesh pebbled her skin.

"Let's get you out of the water."

She nodded. Her teeth chattered. "I'm freezing, but I'm so incredibly warm."

He smiled, then kissed the tip of her nose. "Amazing how that happens, isn't it?"

"Oh, Ben. I never knew." Tears glistened in her eyes. "I never knew."

He hadn't known, either.

9

BEN IDLED HIS STINGRAY at the corner of Cherry and Elm. Heidi lived three houses down on the left. He could see her place, which meant, if she was looking, she could see his car. Because of that, he hesitated to turn.

She was going to kill him for coming here. Nobody came here. She'd warned all of them—him and Quentin and Randy and Jack—never to come to her house.

But she hadn't been in school today. And she'd missed practice. The Joker never missed practice. She might be late to school, or be out the entire day, but she always showed up at practice.

The afternoons she walked into the band hall when she hadn't been to a single class all day, Mr. Philips never said a word. Other teachers called it skipping, but the band director knew what Ben knew about where Heidi came from. And that she only stayed at home, well, when she didn't have a choice.

Being in school was a lot easier for her than staying at home. And playing in the band was pretty much what she lived for.

Ben worried some on those days when he didn't see her in the morning, locking her bike at the bicycle racks. It was like he'd gotten used to starting his day that way.

But he didn't worry a lot because he knew he'd see her later at practice, when she came in all full of herself and everything. He worried about that, too, sometimes. But he figured it was just her way.

He sighed, knowing he couldn't sit here at the corner forever. Maybe he should've let Quentin do this. Quentin's VW bug would fit into this neighborhood a little better than Ben's 'Vette. The frowns he'd caught since he'd passed over the river made him feel like a specimen or something.

He stayed in low gear to make a slow muffled crawl up the block. He didn't really want to park in the street but his car would bottom out if he hit one of the craters in the Malones' shell-and-gravel driveway. And since the driveway was about ninety-five percent cratered, well, the street would have to do.

Besides, with the ratty old station wagon parked half in the driveway, half in the yard and the refrigerator laying on its side next to black garbage bags bulging with aluminum beer cans, there really wasn't room to park. At least the trash was neat. Probably because of Heidi.

He got out of the car, and found himself matching the steely-eyed glare of the gawking grade-school boy hanging out on the sidewalk next door. "How loud can you whistle?"

The response was shrill and piercing.

Good enough. "Five bucks if you keep an eye on the car."

The boy sauntered over, his hands shoved in pockets of loud red-patterned jams, a skinny rattail hanging long down his back. "Ten, and I'll think about it."

"Seven or I drive outta here."

The boy rolled his eyes, held out his hand. "Seven. In advance."

Ben dug into the pocket of his jeans. "Two in advance. The other five if you're still here when I get back."

The boy grumbled, but snatched the two offered bills. He took up sentry duty on the sidewalk in front of Heidi's house, then circled the 'Vette.

Ben walked over green weeds and brown grass to the concrete slab porch. He knew Heidi's room was actually the attic. He'd been here once—before she'd threatened him within an inch of his life if he ever came back.

He hadn't been upstairs, but he'd seen her through the front dormer window that was open now with a box fan blowing on high. The window up there made it look like the house had two stories. When it really didn't.

He glanced up again as he got closer to the front door. He didn't see her but he knew she was there. He heard the sax, low and mournful, so he knew she was okay. That came as a bigger relief than he'd ever have thought.

He looked back once at the scruffy kid, then turned around and knocked before he changed his mind. Mrs. Malone was slow to open the door. She wore jeans. And her blouse was light green and trimmed down the front with green boa feathers. The TV was loud and her shirt was tangled and Ben didn't want to know what he'd interrupted.

Her eyes were droopy; she smelled like beer. It wasn't like she was drunk so much as it was like she was never sober. From what he'd picked up on when Heidi'd actually mentioned her mother, he figured that was pretty much how it was.

He knew Heidi's mom worked in a bar. When she worked. "Uh, hi. Is Heidi here?"

"In her room." Mrs. Malone jerked a thumb toward the hallway and the attic's pull-down staircase, but she didn't invite him in. She narrowed her eyes until the makeup on her lashes looked like spider legs sticking out at him. "You one of them fancy school boys she knows? You comin' down to the river to have a piece of cheap fun?"

"Uh, no, ma'am." Ben fidgeted from one foot to the other. He really didn't like this. He really should've made Quentin come.

"'Cause if you are..." Mrs. Malone went on as if he'd never opened his mouth. "I gotta tell you that you're sniffin' 'round the wrong kitty cat. My girl knows what she's worth. She's had men offer. And no one's having her 'til I say so."

Anger, fierce and burning, ripped through his stomach. What kind of mother did Heidi have? "She wasn't at school. Or at band practice. I just wanted to make sure she was okay."

Mrs. Malone pushed back a bunch of messy brown hair. Her fingernails were painted bright red. Most of the polish was chipped. "She's been blowing on that damned ol' horn most all of the day, most all of her life if the truth be known. And I tell you what—" She shook a finger at him. "I got a real good ear and I don't know why you rich Johnson boys think she's not good enough, making her practice day after day when I need her here to take care of things. Just look at this place. It's turning into a real pigsty."

No. It wasn't.

It was worse.

"Could I go up and see her now?"

"Upstairs?" she asked like he was out of his mind. "Just the two of you? Hey, Earl. You think my baby girl will be safe with this here Johnson boy?"

Ben heard deep male grumbling and the squeak of sofa springs. This had been such a bad idea. "Maybe you could just ask Heidi to come down?"

Mrs. Malone gave Ben a full head-to-toe once-over. She pulled the edges of her feathers tighter together. Then she lifted her chin. "No. You go on up. Heidi won't be wanting nothin' from the likes of you."

Taking a deep breath, Ben stepped through the door. Mrs. Malone went to close it and stopped.

"Unless..." she began.

Ben waited, watched her eyes widen as she caught sight of his car. When she turned back, her face was softer somehow, her eyes brighter. Shrewd. "What did you say your name was?"

"It's Ben. Ben Tannen."

"Well, Ben." She wrapped one arm around his shoulder. "You go right on up. Stay as long as you need to."

He didn't know which was worse, the cigarettes or the old perfume. Added to the beer she'd been drinking, the smell made him think of old shoes.

"Thanks." He hoped he wouldn't have to stay long at all.

He hurried down the short hallway, heard Heidi's

mother working to rouse the sleeping Earl to, "come see what's sitting out in front of the house."

Great. Just great. He should've paid the kid the ten bucks he'd wanted. And all in advance.

A bare bulb hung in the hallway just behind the attic staircase. The pull-down stairs weren't made for the regular climbing they got judging by the loose braces. Ben wondered if ol' Earl had a screwdriver on him, then decided not to ask.

The attic was bigger than he'd thought it would be. And Heidi had only fixed up a part of it for her room. She'd papered the ceiling with posters attached between rafters, posters of jazz greats. A few Ben recognized, Louis Armstrong, Charlie Parker, and others he didn't have a clue.

She'd also hung a bright tie-dyed sheet across the end of the area she'd partitioned off as her own. The walls had black tar paper covering what insulation was stuffed between the wall studs. She'd given the room a sixties look by splattering bright neon paint from floor to ceiling.

She sat on the edge of her bed, which was really just a mattress and box spring stacked on the floor. She had one bare leg tucked up under her, the other foot flat on the ground while she played. It looked like she wasn't wearing anything but a huge University of Texas football jersey.

He knew she wasn't happy to see him, though she didn't say a word. She didn't have to. The way she was looking at him over the sax with those big angry eyes was enough.

Ben wasn't sure what to do next so he raised his hand in a lame wave and hunkered down to listen.

Heidi closed her eyes and went on to finish the song. It was a sad sound, but she knew how to make the sax sound that way. He wondered if she played what she felt, knew what she did when the notes grew sharp and furious.

The weirdest thing, though, was how he felt watching her. He watched her all the time in practice and in competition, but this was different. He didn't know if it was the music or Heidi, but, man, his heart was pounding in his throat.

Boy, this wasn't turning out the way he'd thought. He'd only come here to make sure she was okay. But here in her room with her clothes and her posters and all of her things, she looked like an ordinary girl instead of The Joker.

The Joker didn't make him this nervous, or make his palms sweat when he looked at her legs. He wanted to say something to her, but he didn't know what to say. And he wanted to tell her a lot of things, but he didn't know where to start.

Her hair had grown out since last year, but it still looked like scarecrow straw. She still never wore makeup, though he didn't know why she would. She had the cleanest skin, the biggest, brownest eyes.

He wondered suddenly if her scrubbed plain face and hayseed hair had anything to do with her mother...and the men. She could never be ugly, even if she tried. Which she did. And now he knew why.

Damn. He felt his hackles rise and his heart was pounding so hard his face had to be lobster-red. How could she live like this?

Yeah, her room was neat, the floor had a big braided rag rug in the middle. Her clothes were folded and stacked inside two vegetable crates, and hung on hangers hooked over a wire stretched catty-corner from the edge of the window to the opposite wall.

Yeah, she had her posters and her privacy and her music. But how could that ever be enough? How could that make up for what he'd seen, oh, cripes, and what he'd heard downstairs? Man, she had to get outta here.

She finished the song, laid the sax across her lap. And then she just looked at him with so much disappointment on her face.

"Your mom said you've been playing that thing all day. Actually," he went on, getting to his feet and walking over to peer out the window, "she said you've been playing all your life." He faced Heidi where she sat on her bed against the opposite wall. "I didn't know you'd been playing that long."

Her gaze fell to the horn in her lap. She touched the keys. "My grandfather played sax. I didn't know him, but my dad used to tell me stories. He'd spin these really old records, ya know? The ones that're all hollow and scratchy sounding? Like the band had been playing inside a tin can?

"Anyway." She gave a quick shake of her head. "I was pretty little, like about four or five. But I remember him talking. His voice was really smooth. And mellow. He'd say, 'Listen here. Now. Right now. Hear that tone? That's your grandpapa. He's playing right there alongside Stan Getz.'

"What did I know about jazz? I just liked the music. It was a great backup for my daddy's voice." She shrugged, reached for the case and methodically stored the sax. "This belonged to my grandfather. It was the last one he played," she said and snapped the case's latch.

Oh, boy. Ben couldn't even find his voice to answer. In those few words Heidi had said more about her life than she'd told him in two years. He wanted to know more about her grandfather. He wanted to ask what had happened to her dad. Had he died? Did he leave?

And, if so, why hadn't he taken Heidi with him, away from this life, this place, this disgustingly depressing existence.

"So you have been playing a long time," was all he could finally get out.

"Longer than you've been beating those drums."

He would've laughed if she'd been kidding, but she was serious as a heart attack. And that really cheesed him off. He'd been stupid for not sending Quentin, stupider for worrying in the first place. Why the hell was he even here?

Bottom line, Ben thought, heading back toward the staircase, Heidi didn't need him. Hadn't ever, wouldn't ever need him. This was just a waste of time and energy. His, Heidi's, and ol' Earl's down there on the couch.

"What're you doing here, Ben?"

Keep walking. Keep walking. He felt her gaze follow him and he stopped. "You weren't at practice. I just came by to make sure you were okay."

"And now that you've seen my life, you can rest assured that I'm never okay."

It was the whisper that got to him. He'd've been okay if she'd shouted or acted out like The Joker did when she was pissed. But soft and small and injured he couldn't deal with. He rubbed a hand over his forehead.

"I'll stay. For a while. If you want me to." He didn't know what else to do.

"No need." She hopped up from the mattress, tugged the jersey down to midthigh. The attitude thing again. "I'm fine. I'll be at practice tomorrow. The lovely Mrs. Malone never locks me up here for more than a day at a time."

Ben spun. Blood rushed to his head. "What? She locks you up here?"

"C'mon, Ben. It's no big deal." Heidi reached for a pair of cutoffs and casually pulled them on beneath her jersey. "It's not like she cuts off my head or anything."

Not a big deal? His ears were burning and his eyes were on fire and she was dressing in front of him and this wasn't a big deal? "What about your hair? She cut that off?"

Heidi fluffed at the bleached-out mess. "No, I do this myself."

"Why?"

"Why do you think?" she asked, her hand slowly coming down from her head, her eyes bright and her voice like a gunshot.

"Because you can't afford a *stylist?*" A mocking word she'd thrown in his face regarding his own precision cut. He didn't want to yell, but he was yelling. He didn't want to care, but he cared.

"Because I can't afford not to."

"What's that supposed to mean?" But he knew. Deep in his sick gut, he'd always known.

"Figure it out, Ben. You're a smart boy. Or you

were until you pulled this stupid stunt. There was a reason I didn't want you to come here. Now you've seen it. Now you can go."

"Heidi—"

She put up a hand, stopping him. "Ben, listen. This isn't *Friday The Thirteenth,* it's my life. And I deal with it, okay? You don't have to."

"This shouldn't be anybody's life."

"Why? Because you're a Tannen and you say so? Because it's unfair? Because it makes you uncomfortable? Why?" Hands in fists at her hips, she leaned toward him and pleaded. "Why can't things just be the way they are because they are?"

He took a minute to breathe so he didn't blurt out words he'd regret. Heidi meant too much for him to have any regrets. "You're smart, Heidi. You're talented. You deserve better."

"Dang it, Ben. You think I don't know that?" Her frustration ran as high as his. She spun a circle where she stood then walked on bare feet toward him.

"You think I don't bust my butt at school and practice for a reason? Two more years." Her voice dropped back down to a whisper as she held her fingers up in a V. "Two more years and I'm gone. I can survive anything for two years."

Growing up like this, living here, like this, how could she be so strong?

"Okay," he said, wishing he wasn't having so much trouble today coming up with things to say. Wishing his throat didn't hurt so much when he said that one single word.

"I'll be fine, Ben. I will because I have to. I have my sax. And I have all of you guys." She was standing in front of him now and she reached out and fingered the placket of his shirt.

And then she hugged him. She just reached her arms up around his neck and pressed her body to his.

She was so small. One hand found and spanned the curve of her waist from her hipbone to her ribs. The other barely fit between her shoulder blades. He'd never thought she was this small. It was like wrapping his arms around nothing.

Until he felt how firm her chest was. The jersey she wore was bulky and big but his hands knew she wasn't wearing a bra. Which made him aware that what he'd thought were buttons or knots of shirt were her nipples.

He groaned. Why did she have to have nipples?

"Ben?" Her breath was warm against his ear.

He grunted. And sounded just like a pervert.

"Promise me something?"

He grumbled out, "Sure. What?"

Her hands moved from his shoulders to his chest. And then she shoved. Hard. And glared up at him to yell in his face.

"Don't you ever come to my house again. Never, ever again!"

HEIDI CAME AWAKE slowly, squinting against the morning light, but not opening her eyes. She forced down a yawn and breathed evenly, hating to move too soon and risk waking Ben.

His breathing remained even and deep and stirred the hair at her nape—quite a far cry from his ragged panting which had heated her skin only hours ago.

Twelve hours ago she'd been a virgin and now she

was not. What had they been thinking last night? Doing it in public? Scant yards away from prying eyes in formal wear?

The better question was, had they been thinking at all? Or had they only been feeling, acting on age-old urges and fantasies? She hadn't even fulfilled the promise she'd made to herself and settled the issue of the assault before getting physical, dang it.

Sex in a swimming pool was hardly the deflowering she'd imagined. Even if deflowering by Ben had always been a secret, okay, warped, flight of fancy she'd not even shared with Georgia. And waiting until the age of thirty-three to have sex had never been any sort of grand plan.

If she'd fallen in love, if she'd found a man with whom she wanted to spend her life, whose children she wanted to carry, a man who made her laugh and made her burn and filled her days with happiness and joy and, above all, love, she'd never have given a second thought to sleeping with Ben Tannen.

But she'd rarely dated. And Ben had been constantly and naturally on her mind, working through her college years, as she'd done when she was able, in order to repay his loan.

She'd been career obsessed, with university and law school, the grunt work of internship, the junior partnership at the firm where she'd met Georgia and their dual fate had been sealed.

Heidi sighed and behind her, Ben stirred. His knee nudged the side of her thigh and she smiled at the brush of his hair on her skin. She melted back into his body and he held her there with one arm.

Snuggling and seeking his warmth, she promised

herself no regrets. Her fantasy had become her reality. Whatever this meant to Ben, the night had been beautiful, an experience she'd never forget.

And a measure to which she'd always hold physical relationships.

There were too many women who didn't know this tenderness, who knew only violence and poverty and abuse. She had been one of them.

The first case she and Georgia had worked on together, the case that had taken them from co-workers to partners in their own fledgling firm, had involved a seventeen-year-old client wanting to be declared a legal adult to escape an abusive father.

She was going to kill him, the girl had said, if she had to stay there and fight off his sexual advances, she was going to kill him. The teen had reminded Heidi so much of herself with her ill-fitting clothes and chopped hair and her attitude.

She'd been scrappy and independent and Heidi had done what no attorney should do and let her personal agenda color her arguments on the girl's behalf, color her condemnation of the system, as well—a system which had never conducted an inquiry into a minor child's pleas.

The strong-arm legal team had won, and Heidi had known a personal fulfillment she'd been waiting for all of her life. She'd stood in the courtroom while it emptied and then she'd cried buckets of silent tears until she was spent. Until her throat swelled unbearably and the knot of fire in her stomach burned in her chest.

She'd known then that she was going to make a difference. And she had.

She *would* spend her life working to prove that decency and respect were basic human rights, not benefits to be earned.

To prove that belonging and acceptance and opportunity were not issues of money or class or genealogy, but of qualification and competency.

To prove to Ben that she'd been worthy of his friendship, that his investment had been money well spent.

Her eyes flew open. She stared at the white boards of his bedroom's tongue-and-groove ceiling. No. She had nothing to prove to Ben. Nothing.

And, no, she hadn't given him her virginity to settle her IOU. If that's what he thought, well, she'd straighten that out and quick.

Years ago they'd made a devil's bargain. He'd offered her the money she needed to get into the school of her choice, enough money for books and essentials and, incredibly, enough money to live on campus away from home.

And she'd accepted his offer. How could she say no? She'd been desperate to escape the hellish situation she lived in, desperate to begin her education. A degree was her only ticket out, her only prospect for a future in the world beyond the river.

She'd been so humiliated. Taking money from a friend? She'd rather have taken it from a stranger. Anything would've been better than having to face Ben, to see the pity in his eyes, to see him look at her like she was nothing.

Because in that moment when he'd handed her the check, she'd been less than nothing.

He'd saved her life with the offer and what had she done? She'd flayed his face.

And later, she'd written the note, promising him his money's worth, feeling like a double-whammy disgrace, first for taking the cash, second for making the offer.

But she knew from her mother's example what women did in exchange for men's money. She didn't understand then about friendships. She certainly didn't understand about love. She'd just known that she owed Ben more than simple interest.

And the longer she lay here in his bed, his body warm and comforting against her back, and reflected on what she'd done fifteen years ago in the context of what she'd done last night, the more restless and uncomfortable she grew.

They still hadn't talked about the assault. Or about why he'd brought her home. Besides the sex. If there was anything *besides the sex*. Heidi stopped the nervous tap of her fingers against the side of the bed and thought about the sex.

They'd made it undetected out of the pool last night. Returning to the party, however, had been out of the question, what with damp hair, makeup ravaged by chlorine and kisses, wet or absent underwear.

As it was, she cringed at the thought of her thong, which they'd never been able to find in the water, being discovered today by the maintenance man.

This morning she was sore and she was sensitive and she ached and felt rubbed raw. Ben hadn't pressed for more once they'd made it to his house. He'd urged her instead to sleep.

But she'd wanted him again. She loved the feel of him filling her. And he'd filled her long into the night, discovering what touches she liked and where, the pressure that drove her crazy, how his tongue could make her insane.

Showing her what she could do to send him over the edge.

That had been what she'd most enjoyed, learning his body, how to bring him to incoherent pleasure until he quivered beneath her hands.

He'd teased her about being an apt and eager pupil. She'd countered that he was a patiently precise and very horny professor.

Shifting onto her back, she stretched her arms above her head, feeling the twinges and stings and remnants of achy muscles in her stomach and her thighs. She ran the sole of her foot over Ben's naked calf.

Lying beside him like this, waking in the morning to remember the long passionate night would be so easy to get used to. But she could hardly expect anything more than this weekend when they both led such busy lives.

Love conquers all, Heidi. Ha! Who said Ben loved her? Randy, the rat, had teased her, but she hadn't taken him seriously—at least, no longer than it had taken her to remember to breathe.

Yes, Ben had made love to her, made love with her, but all that had been resolved during the hours of the night was her incomplete sexual education.

Did she love Ben? Was she in love with him? Would she know the difference?

Right now she couldn't fathom never seeing him

again because he was so close she could feel every beat of his heart, the brush of his chest hair on her back with every breath he breathed.

But she was due in court tomorrow...she'd be going back to Dallas today... She just couldn't let herself believe this was anything more than a moment out of time, she couldn't let herself believe they had any sort of future.

She'd never expected any of her dreams to come true. She'd only used them to survive. And right now survival meant pulling back, not getting her hopes up.

Because no matter what she believed to be right, no matter all that she'd fought for, she'd never be good enough for the love of Ben Tannen.

10

WHEN BEN AT LAST came fully awake, Heidi was in the shower. He hadn't heard so much as the squeak of a spring when she'd finally left his bed. No wonder. With the night he'd had, he'd been out like a light.

Not so earlier this morning. He'd spent more than a few minutes drifting in and out of consciousness listening to her think.

She'd tried so hard to be quiet and he had to give her credit. She really hadn't made any audible noise. But her thoughts made her heart beat faster, forced her breathing to stop and start with each shift in mental gears.

He'd come close to making love with her then. Nothing like a good orgasm for stress relief—especially with a stress level near peak capacity. But he wasn't a total jerk. He knew her body needed healing time.

Even now, lying beneath nothing but a white cotton tent, er, sheet, picturing her under the spray of the shower, soapsuds slithering down her limbs, over her torso and the swell of her rump, he had the most basic urge to join her.

To stand below the water's steamy blast and fog up the bathroom mirror with their shared body heat. Instead, he stowed his "camping gear" and forced himself from bed.

Snagging up a pair of sweats, he headed to the upstairs guest bath. The wooden flooring creaked beneath the slap of his bare feet and he stopped to straighten the last in the row of framed quilt squares Mrs. Jones had hung the length of the hallway wall.

When he'd bought this old farmhouse he'd modernized the plumbing and upgraded the ancient water heater. So, Heidi running out of hot water while he showered wasn't a worry—not with his spray running on the cool side of frigid.

He did, however, worry about Heidi running out on him. It seemed to have become her pattern. He was surprised she hadn't jumped in one end of the pool last night, come up for air on the other side and kept going.

Why was she always running? What was she so compelled to run from? For a long time he'd thought her initial flight had been because of his money, her lack and the embarrassment of that whole scenario.

But she should've gotten beyond that by now, being such a woman of substance. He worked his thoughts and his shampoo into a lather. The Mighty Heidi Malone was the embodiment of The Joker's potential. She was strong and she was capable. He scrubbed harder at his hair.

My God, look where she'd come from, what she'd made of herself in the years since she'd left Sherwood Grove. Was it the return to this place where she'd grown up that had her running scared? Soap in hands, he came to a screeching mental stop.

Bingo.

Think about it, Ben. Coming to grips with where he'd come from had begun with a similar trip home. It wasn't that much of a leap to see how the same could be happening to Heidi this weekend.

Especially when he considered that her flight of years ago had probably saved her life. And still she'd come back. For him. She'd made love with him. She'd given him her virginity.

And she'd done it beneath the same urban roof where she'd once been locked in an attic to secure her chastity.

What a sick, twisted world.

He felt the change in pressure as Heidi turned off her water. He shut off his own shower and quickly toweled dry. Working still-damp legs into his sweats, he hurried back to his room prepared to bar the door.

She wasn't leaving until they had talked about last night, about high school, about why each time he moved closer she ran in the other direction. Amazingly enough, he made it in time.

She hadn't left, but he wasn't at all surprised to find her packing the overnighter she'd brought in from her car last night.

Neither was he amused. "You don't waste any time, do you?"

She raised her freshly scrubbed face. No makeup, just faded jeans, Nikes and a T-shirt condemning the banning of books.

Pushing damp ringlets away from her face, she twisted her hair into a careless knot and secured it with a chopstick.

Only then did she plant her hands at her hips and glare. "Why do you say that? Because I have a long drive and need to get my act on the road? Or because I thought it best to be covered before you came back to the room?"

Her honesty surprised him. And, yeah, it aroused him as well, so sue him. "Can't keep your hands off me, huh?"

"It's not my hands I'm worried about," she grumbled, reaching for the shoes she'd worn to the party last night and tucking them into her bag.

Ben's tension eased even as it intensified. Heidi seemed a reluctant victim of the "wanna stay, but gotta go" scenario. And he would've bet it was the first part giving her the most trouble. She was none too happy about wanting to stay, while he could hardly keep from rubbing his hands with glee.

He grabbed a T-shirt from his dresser drawer, slipped his bare feet into old canvas boat shoes. Then he headed for the bedroom door. "Let's go."

She crossed her arms over her chest and looked like she was sixteen years old again. "Let's go?"

"I'm starved. And Mrs. Jones makes apple pancakes like you wouldn't believe. Besides," he added, feeling ruthless in his ploy to keep her from leaving. "You told me you wouldn't run out on me. Ever again."

"I'm not running out on you." She couldn't finish her argument. Not when her voice sang with guilt. Leaving behind her bag and her attitude, she tentatively walked toward him. "But I am hungry. And I don't think I've ever had an apple pancake in my life."

Such an easy victory. He didn't even bother to

gloat. But he did turn up the charm. "Don't tell me you've turned into a fruits and nuts kinda girl."

"Not really." She followed him down the stairs. "I'm more the no-time-for-breakfast kinda girl."

"Well, this morning you have plenty of time." He'd make sure of that. "And if you aren't sure about the apples, her second best offering is pecan."

They stepped into the kitchen just as Mrs. Jones took up the last of the mesquite-smoked bacon from a cast-iron skillet. The line of her mouth wasn't as much disapproving as it was disappointed, no doubt because she'd had to wait this long to meet the first woman Ben had ever brought home.

"Mornin', folks. Bacon's hot, coffee's steamin'. And pancake batter's just waitin' for your order."

Ben walked up behind the feisty woman, tugged on her apron strings. "Mrs. Jones. I want you to be the *first* to meet an old friend of mine, Heidi Malone."

"An old friend, huh? It wouldn't hurt none to let me know when you're having company." Mrs. Jones shook her paring knife at Ben. He dodged, snatched away the coil of apple peel dangling from her other hand. "And an overnight guest at that. Did you at least put out clean towels? And a fresh bar of soap?"

"Yes," he hedged. He didn't know what towels Heidi had used. "Clean towels and the soap was fine. And if I'd known Heidi was coming home with me, I would've let you know."

"You have a phone in that truck of yours. Sherwood Grove is forty minutes away. Don't make excuses." Mrs. Jones didn't put up with nonsense. Shaking her head, she turned to Heidi. "I don't know where he learned his manners."

Heidi pulled out a straight-back chair from beneath the long pine table and perched on the edge. She nodded her enthusiastic agreement. "His conduct does need work, you're right. Can you believe that he left the dance last night without a good-bye or a thank-you to anyone?"

Mrs. Jones clicked her tongue, picked up the batter and stirred. "Shameful. Plain shameful."

Ben leaned back against the sink's edge, arms and feet both crossed. Planning his counterstrike, he lifted a brow. "You said we couldn't go back. Not when you were all wet."

Mrs. Jones stopped stirring. "Wet?"

"Sprinklers. For the rose gardens. At the club." Heidi blushed like a lying ex-virgin then glared at Ben. "I doubt Mrs. Jones is really interested in our night."

"Right now the only thing I'm interested in is hearing how you take your pancakes."

"Apple sounds wonderful, thank you." Heidi released a long sigh.

"Apple it is. Ben, don't just stand there like you're too much of a man to help in the kitchen. Get Miss Heidi a cup of coffee."

Mrs. Jones stirred fresh apple shavings, cinnamon and sugar into the bowl. "You can tell me all about the party later. Because I do believe it has the sound of a story that could take awhile."

"So, THE JONESES don't know about The Deck?" Heidi asked, looking up at him from the bottom of the back porch steps. "Or anything that went on at Johnson High?"

This morning she'd found out that Mrs. Jones made a breakfast hard to turn down. And hard to walk away from. Now Ben was taking her to the barn to see Charlie's new foal. And to meet Thackery.

So far they hadn't even made it off the back porch. Heidi had stopped to rub the furry belly of his big dog named Lug, and the cats had descended like ants on a picnic, from beneath the porch, out of the barn, down from the huge oak that shaded the house.

Ben might have to watch where he put his feet, but he wasn't going to back away from the subject they'd been sidestepping all weekend. In fact, he stopped his descent on the last step and, making an effort to keep the weight from a heavy subject, plunged teasingly in.

"You mean, do the Joneses know you're the one who turned my face into this hideously gruesome visage? That you stole away every chance I had to be *People Magazine*'s 'Sexiest Man Of The Year'?"

She rolled her eyes. "A little scar never stopped Harrison Ford."

"You call this little?"

At his words, she straightened, climbed two steps to take his chin in her hand. She turned his head this way then that. The chain had dented the center of his chin, leaving a Michael Douglas cleft.

She placed the pad of her index finger there, then made a long slow tactile exploration along the curve of his jaw to his ear. She was gentle. She was tender. He watched the scroll of her thoughts in her eyes.

The strip of pale skin was basically smooth, the white line narrow and bare where the bristle of beard should've grown. Her swing had missed both his eye and his ear. He saw her visually measure the distance, saw her register, for the very first time, that her careless heated actions could've cost him either.

Her breath caught. Her eyes brimmed with tears she'd yet to release. His gut clenched hard. Trembling, her hand found its way to his nape. She pulled his head down to trail healing kisses along the injury he'd suffered at her hand.

"Why, Ben?" she whispered at his ear, her breath warm, the dampness of tears on his cheek warmer still. "Why did you tell me to swing?"

He laughed weakly. "I didn't think you would for one thing."

She pulled back to look at him and her throat worked hard as she tried to swallow.

"You were hurting, Heidi. Hurting bad. If you hadn't struck out, you'd've turned all that anger inside." He raised her chin, looked into her eyes. "That scared me even more than the idea of you hitting me."

He'd told her that day that he knew her well. She hadn't wanted to believe him. In their four years of high school, she'd never allowed anyone close. Later, with his arrogance tempered by maturity, he'd realized why she'd kept herself separate.

Her ability to make it from day to day had been steel-forged in her independence. In the way she'd learned never to ask, never to take. And, above all, never to need, as if she'd lose the very tenuous hold she had on the controlling strings of her life if she even thought she had anyone to lean on.

Watching her now, waiting for her to answer, he

had more than a suspicion that she still practiced that philosophy.

"I shouldn't have hit you." She tucked her hands in her jeans pockets and moved down one step. "It didn't matter that I needed to 'strike out', as you say. I shouldn't have hit you."

"I'm not going to disagree with you there." He didn't want her to sink into a morass of guilt and remorse. So he laughed. "Of course, I'm not sure I would've wanted you to take out your frustration on my 'Vette either."

But her emotions ran too far in the other direction. She was remembering and reliving and regretting. He knew that when she turned away to hide and he felt the first stirrings of his own frustration. He'd gotten over the incident long ago. She needed to get over it now.

She sank down to sit on the step, buried her face in her hands. "Why are you even talking to me now? And, oh, God, Ben. Why did you want to make love with me? After what I've done? I can understand if it was the IOU, but if it wasn't...then what...why?"

Explaining why meant he'd have to deal with the emotions he'd suppressed last night. Funny, but he was finally ready. "We have a history, Heidi. You're not a random classmate I hit on for a little one-on-one reunion." He paused, dropped down to the step above her. He braced his elbows on his knees, tickled the head of the kitten who settled between his feet. "Do you remember what I told you last night?"

She sniffed. "Which what?"

He chuckled. He had been rather mouthy. "That who I am today has a lot to do with you."

Denying his words with a shake of her head, she said, "I don't believe that."

He shrugged. "You don't have to. I do. Oh, I would've said you were full of crap if you'd asked me five years ago."

Her head came up. "So what's different now?"

"Me. I am."

This time she looked at him, raised that cocky Joker's brow. "That's it?"

He nodded. "Five years ago, I came home. To Sherwood Grove. Things weren't going well for me and Katherine. I couldn't say why. Just that I didn't feel a part of 'us.' I didn't belong. Or fit in."

"Don't patronize me, Ben."

The return of Mighty Heidi. Even better. "Fine. Here's this." He made sure he had her full attention, that her eyes were focused on his. "There hasn't been a day of my adult life that I haven't thought about you. They weren't always nice thoughts, either."

"What did you think about me, Ben?"

Her eyes were bright and dry. Her curiosity piqued. Her voice had taken on the tenor of cross-examination. Suddenly all this honesty didn't seem like such a good idea.

At the rumble of the kitten's purr, Ben glanced down. Eyes slashed shut, the tiny feline settled her triangular head on his foot. His mind was in chaos and the cat was asleep.

"Ben?"

I hear ya, counselor. "What did I think? I hated you and damned you and worried and wondered. More than anything, I wondered."

"About?"

"How you survived. You lived by the river in a house of tar paper and trash. I lived in the heart of Sherwood Grove with servants and chandeliers. You rode a five-speed with one working gear to school. I drove a Corvette. You had nothing compared to my everything. Yet I didn't have half your self-sufficiency.

"I did what was expected of me instead of thinking for myself. I had it good. I had it great, in fact." He shrugged, trying to dislodge the weight that had descended when she'd turned the questions on him. "Why put out any effort to change?

"Then I thought of you. Living the way you did. Doing what you had to do to survive. Sure, we fought and argued like all kids do, but you never did anything, said anything that couldn't be worked out with a game of pool and a lot of loud music.

"I didn't think anything about giving you that money. That's just how Tannens did things. 'A problem? No problem. Name your price and it's history.'" How many times had that scenario been played out in his father's library?

He looked into Heidi's eyes then, because this was what he'd been waiting fifteen years to make right. "It took me less than a minute to write out a check and hand you what you'd spent your entire life working for. I didn't think about your feelings. And that was wrong."

She was frowning, shaking her head adamantly. "But if you hadn't given it to me..."

"I've thought about that, too. If I hadn't, would you be where you are today?" A second kitten joined the first and the tickle to his toes intensified. "I've also wondered how things might've been different if I'd offered you the loan. If we'd talked about it. If I hadn't arrogantly assumed I could solve your problems with my bank account."

Gently lifting a snoozing feline in each hand, he reached back and set them in a quiet corner of the porch. They blinked, glanced around then were up and off, tumbling to the ground before tearing across the yard toward the barn. Ben rolled his eyes. "Ingrates."

Heidi laughed. And then she said, "You did solve my problems, you know. If not for you, I doubt I'd've ever made it to the other side of the river."

No. He couldn't take the credit. "You were strong, Heidi. You'd've made it just fine."

"I don't think so. I'd reached the end of my rope that day." Leaning toward him, she placed her hand on his knee. "When you drove up to the bike racks, I'd been thinking about what I was going to do. I'd been holding on for so long, you know. Waiting to get out of school and out of that place.

"But all of a sudden the only thing I could see was the end. Of my future. My chances. Of my life," she said and her voice dropped.

"It wasn't where I lived, the house or the neighborhood. It was my situation. I saw myself becoming my mother." She looked down at her feet. "Taking money from men to survive. Up until that day I never thought I'd sink to that level..."

Ben squeezed his eyes shut and hung his head. He'd never thought about that. Why in the hell had he never thought about that? "I did that to you. That's why you sent me that note."

Her nod was an admission. "And then when you called, I thought you wanted to collect." She laughed. "I didn't know what to do. I'd never thought you'd actually take me up on it. I figured you hated me. That you'd never want to see me again much less..."

"Make love with you? That note wasn't about making love. I might only have been nineteen when you sent it, but I knew that much at least. The note pissed me off. I came close to hating you then. But I called because I wanted to make sure you were doing okay.

"When you wouldn't even talk to me, well, yeah. That's when I thought about using that note against you. I was young and arrogant and convinced you owed me more than money. But most of my anger came from seeing you living your dream while I was living the life expected of a Tannen."

Her smile was thoughtful, gentle. "And now?"

Ah, that was easy. "Now I'm living for me."

She squeezed his knee, patted his thigh then clasped her hands together. "I just can't believe you didn't forget about me the minute you hit the UT campus."

"I told you, Heidi. I think about you every day." He turned his scarred face toward her. "How can I help it?"

"Ben." She moved to sit at his side, to wrap both arms around him and hold him close. "I am so incredibly sorry. I don't even know what to say."

His heart beat faster. "Tell me one thing."

"Anything," she whispered.

"Did you forget about me?"

She shook her head. "Never."

"And now? Where do we go from here?" He

clenched and unclenched his hands. This was the hardest question of all because he was not going to let her walk out of his life. Not after this weekend.

Not when he loved her.

"From here?" Her eyes were bright and dreamy when she said, "I'd like to go back to your bed."

SHE UNDRESSED HIM slowly, taking her time with discovery and exploration. His body was beautiful, a work of art worthy of Michelangelo. Sculpted of stone, the master's David couldn't have felt so smooth, so hard.

Ben's shoulders were beautifully wide and strong. She knew their strength from the way he effortlessly held his body above hers when he strained for control. She dropped his T-shirt to the floor and let her hands roam.

His skin was familiar, but she refused to rush what might never come again. So, his biceps, his elbows, his forearms and wrists and palms and fingers received her attention. Each inch of skin, every mole, every freckle, every scratch and scrape and bruise.

Tenderly, gently, thoroughly she grew to know him. These were the arms that had held her close in the night, the hands that had braced her for ecstasy, the fingers that had wiped away the tears of joy her best intentions could not contain.

"Heidi?"

She looked up from the broad palm she was measuring with the press of her thumb. His eyes were the eyes she'd seen in her dreams for more than half of her life.

"I'm six feet tall. I weigh one hundred eighty

pounds and I wear a size twelve shoe. If you plan to take this long on every inch of me, we're going to be here for a very short time."

"Why not a very long time?"

"Because at this rate I will be over and done with before you even reach my pants."

"Oh," she said and ran the flat of her palm across his bold arousal to see for herself.

Ben hissed out a long breath between clenched teeth. "What're you doing?"

Playing the vamp was even more fun when she wasn't playing. "Just checking to see what will soon be coming my way."

As groans went, Ben's was tortured. "Funny girl."

"The Joker at your service," she said and opened her mouth against the center of his chest.

Skin shouldn't be strong, but that's exactly how she thought of Ben's. A strength of health and conditioning. And he tasted exactly as she remembered.

While making tiny laps with her tongue on his skin, from nipple to nipple to breastbone to his neck, where she left a tiny lover's mark, she walked her fingers beneath the elastic of his sweats and encountered no underwear.

She squeezed the toned flesh of his buttocks and felt the need to press her thighs tight together to hold back her own rush of heat.

"Heidi?"

"Hmm?" she mumbled. She couldn't talk with her tongue wrapped around his nipple. She'd been thrilled to see his response, to know he shared that point of stimulation.

"You're moving faster, baby. And that's a good

thing. But the parts you're moving toward are in an even bigger hurry."

His impatience thrilled her. She wanted him as mindless as she'd been when he'd finally entered her in the pool last night. "You don't believe that patience is a virtue?"

"I believe that good comes aren't for those who wait."

She groaned. "Funny man."

"You're rubbing off on me."

"I'm rubbing on to you."

"So rub more already."

"I hate to rush. I'd like to linger."

"I hate it when you linger. Faster, deeper, harder. That's my motto."

"Ben, you are such a guy."

"I certainly hope so."

"So, act like a guy and kiss me senseless."

She didn't have to ask him twice. His lips pressed hers and his tongue stroked hers and his hands worked her T-shirt up to her shoulders and off her arms. His hands found her breasts, cupped and fondled and squeezed.

She gasped when his mouth took over, sucking hard. She arched toward him, her hands gripping his biceps as he bent her back over his arm. She gave herself up because she had realized last night that there was nothing that drove her as thoroughly wild as his mouth on her breasts.

Except for his mouth on her stomach. She moaned as he kissed his way to her navel, plying the flat of his tongue to her skin. The pressure tickled and aroused and the room's cool air on the hot moisture of his mouth hardened more than her nipples.

She couldn't wait for him to take off her pants. To move his tongue the way that he did between her legs. To tickle her thighs with butterfly kisses, to draw on her feminine flesh with his lips.

His fingers were finally at her zipper and he was skimming her jeans over her hips and lowering her back onto the thick quilted coverlet. And suddenly she stopped him, because she wanted to see him in broad daylight, to watch his face as her mouth made love to him.

He frowned when she pushed him back, a frown that grew panicked as she sat up, found the waistband of his sweats and flicked her tongue over his navel as she freed him from his clothes.

Then she kissed him where it counted and exalted in the response of his body, the heat of his ragged breath, the moans that began belly deep to squeeze his chest, the crush of his hands in her hair and the pulse she measured with her tongue.

But he wasn't having any more of that and when she looked up into his eyes he pulled free of her mouth and tumbled her back onto the bed. He made swift work of whatever clothing still hung from ankles and knees and then he was over her, entering her, burying his body deep within hers.

He loved her slowly, moving nothing but his hips, then refusing to move at all when she squirmed and begged and slapped his butt. His chuckles vibrated through her breasts and he kissed her gently, capturing her hands above her head.

Then he began the true torture, refusing to give up

her mouth, denying her use of her hands and moving his knees to the outside of hers. He started with long slow strokes, withdrawing from her body completely, then easing the whole of his length back in.

How unfair that he treat her this way, holding her still for this intense pleasure. Mind-blowing. She'd heard that term used in reference to sex. She'd scoffed. But now she knew. Ben had reduced her to nothing but feeling, nerves and skin and warm wet friction.

She ripped her mouth free because her release rejected silence. This was love and it was loud and liquid, with sticky moist skin and grunts and whimpers and nasty words and moans. This was love and she was making it with Ben, with her mouth and her fingers and her thighs and her sex.

But most of all, more than anything in the world, she was making it with her heart.

11

Senior year

HEIDI WONDERED what a straight shot of bourbon would feel like going down. If it would drown out the embers sizzling away the lining of her stomach.

Or if it would just go ahead and take away the rest of everything she cared about.

After the day she'd just had, the four years she'd just finished, numbness seemed like a great way to spend the rest of her life.

No more hurt, no more humiliation and certainly no more hope.

Slamming her high school locker closed for the very last time, she pulled her daddy's creased and battered brown derby low over her ears and pushed forward through the rowdy crowd of Johnson High graduates.

The class of 1984.

Notebook paper in balls and sheets, shreds of book covers and strips of crepe paper streamers littered the hallway along with snapshots and sketches and magazine covers and calendars all ripped from locker walls.

The floor was a mess beneath the trampling feet. Heidi felt just as stepped on.

Reaching the end of the senior hallway and the door, she shoved through into the bright May afternoon. The sunlight blasted down, adding fire to the fuel in her belly.

The letter crushed in her hand wasn't helping any, so she shoved it into her satchel.

One more letter to add to the *we're sorry to inform you* stack of financial aid rejections stuffed between her mattress and box springs.

Her counselor had been so certain this last-chance application to this last-chance institution would answer her prayers.

Now Heidi's last chance was a fat chance.

She'd desperately needed this student loan, dang it, any student loan, to meet the costs left uncovered by the few grants that had miraculously materialized.

But she came from the river. And her mother was an unemployed drunk with a credit report worthy of a good flush down the toilet.

The amount of money she'd applied for wasn't a large sum. It really wasn't. But the money men looked at so many things. Things like the fact that with her family history she wasn't a good risk.

Her grades had been decent, but not stellar. Her attendance pretty much the same. The only extracurricular activity on her record was band.

She'd won awards, sure, but awards didn't go far on a credit check. On top of that she'd never held a job and her mother rarely did.

And she was surprised she'd been turned down?

She cut around the teacher's parking lot and trudged toward the bicycle racks behind the school.

Ha. The surprise was that she'd actually made it to her senior year, what with the odds against her.

Hell, during her four years at Johnson High, there'd never even been but a dozen or so bikes chained up to the metal pipes next to hers. Johnson just wasn't that type of school. It was a Camaro school. A TransAm school.

A Corvette type of school.

She'd been so stupid to come here. She could've lied about her address and gone to school with most of the kids who lived down by the river. Like anyone in the system would've cared enough to check that she'd crossed the dreaded boundary lines.

But she'd thought that those who held the purse strings might take her high school into consideration. That at Johnson she'd have a better chance for escape.

Right. She'd just escaped from a four-year-long dream. Now she'd be going nowhere but to a home that wasn't one and a future postponed indefinitely.

Think, Heidi, think. Okay. Tomorrow she'd start looking for a summer job. Between now and August she should be able to earn enough money for the community college's fall semester and get a head start on the costs for the spring.

She was eighteen, she was out of school. Her mother would no longer forbid her from working. Of course, she could kick her out of the house.

But Heidi doubted that would happen. Not when her mother had been waiting for the day when Heidi could finally contribute to the household income.

This was where it was going to get tricky, she realized, slapping her satchel against the bike's pannier. But, dang it, she had to make it work.

She had to find a job that would earn her enough money to save for school, enough extra to help with the rent and the beer, enough hours to keep her away from the house.

Away from the mother who'd insist she was now old enough and educated enough to attract the type of man who'd pay well for her virginity, who'd continue to pay as long as Heidi made him happy.

Oh, that was a life she was looking forward to, Heidi thought, yanking the chain from between the spokes on her wheels. Oh, yeah. Her future really looked bright.

She heard the low rumble of a car approach behind her and stood. No way. She was *not* in the mood. Not now. Not ever again. School was over. And as far as she was concerned, The Deck was history.

Silently she waited for Ben to drive on, drive away, drive off to wherever it was legitimate Johnson High grads celebrated their last day of high school.

Heidi snorted. She'd be surprised to find out Ben wasn't having a pool party and even more surprised if Maryann Stafford hadn't bought a new two-piece for the occasion.

The Corvette stopped and the door opened and Ben killed the engine. The silence made it easier to hear the thoughts which were now screaming at the top of their lungs to be heard.

That picture made Heidi laugh. Thoughts with lungs. Screaming. Which meant they had mouths and voices as well. Did they have feet, too? As many as a centipede?

Is that why there was such a racket in her head? All

these big-mouth thoughts running around screaming hysterically on hundreds of feet?

She'd gone absolutely buggers. Out of her mind certifiably nuts. She doubled over to keep her stomach from reminding her that she hadn't eaten lunch. To keep it from turning inside out at the truth.

Her life had just bottomed out.

"Heidi? You okay?"

Sure. If contemplating what the earth looked like from six feet below counted. She straightened, kept her eyes on the ground. "Just looking for my contact lens."

"I didn't know you wore contacts."

She rolled her eyes his way. Why did he have to look so good? "I don't. What do you want?"

Confusion passed through Ben's green eyes. "I didn't know if, well, a bunch of kids are coming over and we're gonna swim and just chill and watch MTV and stuff."

"Yeah? And?" Why couldn't he just say it and be done with it? And why did she feel this ugly urge to give him a hard time?

"You don't have to be such a bitch." Ben shoved his hands in his jeans pockets and shrugged. "I just thought you might want to come over."

Heidi scowled. She was in such a mood for a fight. "Why would I want to come over when you think I'm a bitch?"

"I don't think you're a bitch—"

"You just called me one."

"I said you were acting like one."

"No. You said I was being one."

Ben scrubbed a hand back over his hair. This year

fashion called for tightly cut sides and length in back and of course Ben had answered. "Look, Heidi. Whatever's bugging you—"

She laughed. "Bugging me. That's funny."

Ben didn't seem to think so. "Do you want to come over or what?"

"How will I get there?"

He looked at her bike. "You can ride with me and pick up your bike later."

She'd never ridden in his Corvette. "I don't have a swimsuit."

"I can take you home to get it."

Her chest rose and fell harder as she spit it out again. "I said, 'I don't have a swimsuit.'"

"Oh, well." He shifted from one foot to the other. "There're always extras in the pool house."

Hand-me-downs. She didn't have anything against them. Except when they came from a Tannen. "I think I'll pass."

"Suit yourself," he said, but then came right back with, "What're you going to do?"

She shrugged. "Same thing I do every day after school. Go home."

"Cripes, Heidi. You can't just go home. You have to celebrate. To party. There's only one last day of school in your entire life."

Last time I can be sure of a safe place to spend the day. Last time I can be considered a schoolgirl.

Last time I can be comforted by your face, your laugh, your eyes which look at me like I mean something.

"Yeah." She pulled the hat from her head, worked the brim with shaky fingers and prayed he couldn't see the nerves that wouldn't stop. "I can celebrate no more bad news from the counselor's office."

He slowly nodded. "I wondered about that. I saw you in there today. What's up?"

"Not my future, that's for sure."

"Whaddaya mean?"

"Nothing. I don't want to talk about it." She jammed the hat back on her head.

"You never want to talk about it when you want to talk about it." He came closer, stopped when she backed away. "I know that about you."

Her eyes burned. "You think you really know me?"

"Yeah. I do. You can't spend as much time with a person as you and I have spent together and not get to know them."

She didn't want him to know her. She didn't want anyone to know her. "You don't know anything."

"I know that there's no reason for you to go home."

"And there's a reason I should go to your house?" She pressed a finger to her chin. "Let me think. What would that be? Because all my friends are there? Oh, wait. I don't have any friends. So, that can't be it."

"You have friends, Heidi."

"Do I, Ben? Do I really? Let's see. I go to school with a bunch of kids who barely tolerate me. I play in a band with a bunch of kids who have to put up with me."

He shoved a finger in her face. "That's bullshit about band and you know it."

She didn't care what he said or what he thought. She didn't, dammit! She just cared that her entire life was falling apart. "I don't spend hours on the phone talking to anyone about hair and clothes and who lost their virginity last week and is pregnant this week.

"Of course, that would be hard to do anyway when I don't even have a phone. I don't hang out at the mall because I have no one to hang out with, no way to get there, no money to spend."

"Cripes, Heidi. You don't have to have money to hang out at the mall."

She glared at him, she hated him for making nothing out of what he couldn't understand. "You have no idea what my life is like, Ben. So I am not going to listen to anything you say."

"I do know what your life is like, Heidi. I've been to your house, remember? Yeah, one time. But that was plenty. I'm not going to let you stand here and say you don't have any friends. Because you have me. And you have Randy and Quentin and Jack.

"We've asked you a lot of times to hang with us. At the movies, or hell, we could've taken you to the mall. It's not like you had to stay home all the time. Maybe we should've asked you more, but you always said no when we did."

Of course she'd said no. What was the point of even sticking a toe into a world that would toss her back, a world that would only let her in because of who she knew. No. She didn't work like that.

She wasn't going to ride anyone's coattails into a world that wouldn't accept her on her own. She'd always made her own way. She had to. That instinct for survival was all that kept her alive.

"Thank you but no thank you. To the mall, to the movies, to the pool party. I'm going to go home and practice. Maybe I can get a job playing blues in a club, save up my tips, go to law school when I'm thirty."

"I don't know why you didn't apply for a music scholarship."

"A music scholarship would mean I would have to play music. I want to study law, Ben. And I wouldn't have the time to do both. Yes, music has been important."

She couldn't even begin to tell him how important, how playing the sax was sometimes all she had. "But now I want to do more. I want to help others. Not everyone has a sax."

Tears filled her eyes, burned as she tried to hold them back. She didn't want to cry in front of Ben. She didn't want to cry at all. She wanted to scream, to kick the spokes out of her bike, to yank out the straw she called hair.

But she couldn't do any of it in front of Ben. Not with him standing there looking like...a college freshman.

"What do you want me to do, Heidi? What do you want me to say? Tell me how I can help."

"I don't need your charity, Ben. So just take your pool party, your car and your UT tuition and shove it all."

She turned her back on him, straddled the five-speed's crossbar, gripped the handlebars until her fingers went numb. Numb, yes. Numb was good.

She heard Ben's footsteps scrape over loose gravel as he walked back to his car. Finally. She kept her eyes closed until she heard his door open, then waited for it to close. More than anything right now she wanted to get out of here, but she wouldn't leave first. She would not run. Not in front of Ben.

She waited and waited and when the car didn't start she almost turned. But she didn't. And then he was coming back. Oh, no. Why did he have to come back right when she'd let the tears fall?

He approached from her left side.

She grabbed the chain to wrap around her handlebars, but worried it through her hands instead, working it palm to palm from one end to the other, never getting anywhere. And wasn't that just about the way of her life. Never getting anywhere.

She sensed him there and waiting, sensed an uncomfortable impatience, but didn't have the presence of mind to separate her building fury that he was still there from his stubborn refusal to leave.

"What?" she finally screamed, snapping her head up to bite his off. "What do you want? Why are you still here? I told you to leave. I'm not coming to your goddamn party."

Her voice rose with every word until even her blood raced at the speed of a shrieking banshee. Her fingers curled around the chain and held it tight because she had a really sick urge to claw out his rich-boy eyes.

She wanted to make him understand what it was like to be Heidi Malone without pool parties and malls and movies. She wanted to make him hold her, to stroke her hair and soothe the pounding of her heart and tell her everything would be okay.

Tears were streaming down her face, her nose was running. Salt stung her lips and she swiped the back of her hand across her mouth, wiped it on the seat of her jeans.

She was a blurry salty drippy mess when he finally spoke. And then it was only one word.

"Here." He held out a piece of paper.

She eyed it warily. "What is it?"

He waved it at her. "Just take it."

She reached for it, looked at it, forgot how to breathe. It was a check, signed by Ben, made out to her, and it had a whole lot of zeroes under the dollar amount. The zeroes were what got to her the most.

"What am I supposed to do with this?" Her attempt at indifference failed miserably. Her hands shook even more than her voice.

"You're supposed to go to school."

School. This was for school? "This is for school? School? As in college?"

"Unless you want to go back to high school. But I think that's still free."

If high school was free, why had she paid so dearly? An amount that seemed to have more zeroes than this check. But her zeroes wouldn't get her into college.

And this would. Damn him to hell, this would.

She held it out. "I can't take this. I don't want it."

Ben crossed his arms. "I don't care. I want you to have it."

"Why? So your angel wings will have diamond-crusted feathers?"

"Nah. I just want to play drums in heaven's band." He shifted from one foot to the other. "Cripes, Heidi. Give it a rest. The money's part of the trust from my grandfather. I got it when I hit eighteen. It's just sitting there waiting for a worthy cause."

"You think I'm a worthy cause?" Two dozen lending institutions hadn't thought so. The paper rattled in her hand.

"Yeah. Sure. Why wouldn't I?"

"Why would you?"

He took a deep breath and blew it out. "Because you're my friend. And because you need it."

What was he doing? Why was he just standing there doing nothing? He wasn't taking back the check. He was just looking at her as if she was insane.

He wanted insane? She'd show him insane. "How dare you tell me what I need!"

She screamed at him, screamed like her chest had been turned inside out. Sobbed as if she would die if she tried to stop. Her throat was ripped open and her heart was torn apart to bursting.

And it was all his fault.

If he hadn't stopped, she'd have been on her way home. She wouldn't be facing one more chance at the future she so desperately wanted—the worst, most hopeless chance of all because this time she was going to have do the turning down.

She lifted the hand holding the bicycle chain. In the back of her mind she heard Ben tell her to swing, to go ahead and swing. And she would've stopped, but her arm was already moving, her elbow was up and her hand heading his way.

The chain hit the side of his face. She felt the bone give and crack, saw the blood gush, heard his cry as he went down to the asphalt parking lot. He didn't move. He just lay there. Sprawled out and silent and not moving.

Oh, God. Oh, God. What had she done? She jumped on her bike, grabbed the handlebars. One hand held the check. One hand the chain. Her head whipped from Ben to the school to Ben to the road. She couldn't see anything. Her eyes were a mess. Couldn't think anything but, "Run!"

Ride. She had to ride. She pushed down with feet that wouldn't move on a bike that wouldn't move. Brick feet on flat tires. She pedaled harder. She pedaled faster.

Pedal, pedal, pedal, pedal.

Oh, God. Oh, God. What had she done? She huffed and puffed, huffed and puffed. Out of the parking lot, onto the road, past the school.

Pedal, pedal, pedal, pedal.

She was over the railroad tracks and halfway home when she heard the peal of the ambulance. She closed her eyes and kept pedaling.

Pedal, pedal, pedal, pedal.

And she was upstairs in her attic room when she knew that, if the cops didn't show up to drag her away, she was going to cash the check.

12

HEIDI BLEW OUT a dissatisfied breath. "I don't know, Georgia. This subpoena may not be enough."

"C'mon, Heidi." Georgia propped both hands on Heidi's desk and leaned forward. She lifted a wicked brow. "We both know it's not the size of the subpoena. It's how you use it that matters."

Heidi lifted her head slowly and glared up with one eyeball. "That's not funny."

"You would've thought it was funny a month ago," Georgia said, backing away to cross both arms over her chest.

That was true enough. Since Heidi had come back from the reunion in Sherwood Grove, she'd lost her sense of humor. Among other things...

She grimaced. If she'd known sex would turn her into this frustrated ineffective unfocused knot, she'd've never given Ben her virginity. Of course, it wasn't sex, or the lack thereof, that was the issue here.

The issue was loving Ben.

She looked up, smiled extra wide and blinked her eyes theatrically, like the breeze from her lashes would blow Georgia away. "I solemnly swear to do my very best to laugh at all of your funnies from now on."

"Hmph. Sounds like someone needs another reun-

ion. And another tumble with a certain man whose
name has not yet been spoken for these best friend
ears to hear," Georgia said and flounced from Heidi's
office.

"Close the door on your way out," Heidi called.

Georgia did, but stuck her head back in and added,
"You were a lot more fun when you weren't getting
any."

Heidi bolted upright at the slam of the door. She
counted to ten. She breathed deeply, from her dia-
phragm. She even spent three minutes in meditation.

And still she had the jumpiness of a cat on a hot tin
roof. Or a cat on the back porch of a farmhouse. Or a
cat ducking the hooves of a new mother mare.

Charlie Parker. Ben had named his horse Charlie
Parker. That single detail was the most telling of all
that, yes, he had truly forgiven her. The scar was a
physical reminder he'd learned to live with.

But to purposefully name his horse after her favorite saxophonist of all time? Even her brain, so lame of
late, couldn't pass off the obvious as coincidence.

So why all these years after the assault and these
weeks after the reunion was she still unable to forgive
herself? It made her seem so pathetic. And she was
not pathetic.

Her career had given her an enviable reputation.
She had the car and the clothing to make any Sherwood Grove debutante green. These days she never
wanted for money. She could splurge on hair and
nails and travel when in the mood.

And a personal trainer even when not.

But none of that had been her goal. The security,
sure, but not the shallow quest for wealth and afflu-

ence for nothing but wealth and affluence's sake. That was not the criterion by which she wished her success to be measured. It certainly wasn't how she judged her own achievements.

She hadn't worked her butt off for these many years just to gain entrance into the world of the Tannens.

Had she?

Shoving her chair back from her desk, she stood and turned, arms crossed, to stare out the wall of windows overlooking the building's landscaped atrium and the parking lot beyond. She'd come so far from the river kid who'd gone to school with the Sherwood Grove debs.

She'd chosen her field of practice to help others forced by life's vagaries into circumstances similar to the ones she'd lived. She had not for one minute thought that, as a high-profile attorney, her profession would grant her access into a society that had shunned her from day one at Johnson High.

Okay. So maybe that thought had moved into a small corner in the back of her mind. And seeing Maryann Stafford's shock of recognition had admittedly given Heidi a thrill. But those were only by-products. Secondary considerations. Her commitment had more depth than that.

Surely that was obvious to Ben.

Whoa. Wait a minute. What did any of this have to do with Ben?

Face it, Heidi. This is all about Ben.

She leaned her forehead against the cool glass and closed her eyes against the wash of overwhelming truth. She'd never cared what Sherwood Grove society thought about where she'd come from, the way she'd looked, or acted or dressed.

She'd only wanted to please Ben. It had been that way since the very first time she'd walked into the band hall as a high school freshman.

He'd accepted her as an equal that day. He hadn't cared that there wasn't a designer label on a single item of clothing she wore. And he hadn't let the other three look at her as anything but the talent she was.

That day Ben had become as important to her as her dream of one day seeing her name on a business card followed by the word *Esquire*. It wasn't easy to admit that even now. She'd been in denial so long.

The night they'd made love had been a night of sharing more than bodies. They'd shared laughter over the remembered antics of The Deck and quite a few of her tears as they'd talked about her father's death and her life prior to Johnson High.

They'd talked about the past fifteen years of their lives. They'd talked about Ben's future at the *Stonebridge Reporter* and hers with Bonds and Malone, LLC.

But they hadn't talked about a future together. He hadn't said he loved her. And when she'd left the next morning, the only thing he'd said was good-bye.

Somehow, somewhere, she'd failed to please him completely. Refusing to forgive herself for the assault cushioned that blow. With her crime against him standing in the way, she wouldn't have to wonder how she'd failed to meet his standards, or to think *if only things were different* because they weren't.

As long as the assault remained as a boulder between them, the rejection would be in her court. And that would ease the hurt of not having him in her life.

She'd been wrong earlier. She was pathetic.

The door to her office opened and closed.

"Go away, Georgia. I'm busy."

"Busy holding that window in place with your head?"

Ben!

Heidi straightened, stared at his reflection in her office window. Her heart stopped because for a fleeting moment what she saw was the image of the boy she'd fallen in love with. His jeans were stone-washed, his feet shoved into bulky athlete-endorsed high-tops, the collar of his red polo shirt turned up against the back of his neck.

It was the distortion of the glass, she knew, that gave him the look of youth and innocence. Because when she turned there was nothing in his face that reminded her of a boy. Ben Tannen was all man.

He was a man on a mission, intent on their unfinished business. What she saw in the lines at the corners of his eyes wasn't anger as much as frustration, not impatience as much as determination.

But what she saw didn't matter half as much as what she felt. How a thrill raced upward from the base of her spine. How the weight on her shoulders lifted.

Funny how he'd show up just when she'd been thinking of him. She laughed to herself. He could've arrived yesterday or flown in tomorrow and still she would have been thinking of him.

She was always thinking of him.

"Ben. What a surprise." She tented both hands on the edge of her desk. "What're you doing here?"

He walked toward her, stopped on the opposite

side of the Queen Anne desk, rubbed a weary hand across the back of his neck. "I've been asking myself that same question for the past two hundred miles."

Interesting that even he didn't know why he was here. "Did you give yourself an answer?"

He shook his head. "I waited a month as it was. I knew you had a case coming to trial and I didn't want to distract you."

She sighed, nudged at the legal pad on her desk. "I always have a case coming to trial."

The hand at his neck came down to grip the head-rest of her guest chair. "So, no time is a good time?"

"I didn't say that." She would never say that. "It's just that I'm always busy."

"Always busy," he repeated. "And that translated from lawyerspeak means too busy?"

"Too busy for some things. Not too busy for others," she said and attempted a smile.

"Too busy to call a friend?"

She shook her head. "No. Not at all. In fact, I called Quentin this past...weekend." The tail of the sentence drifted as she realized where this was going.

"I see." The long lashes of his green eyes barely filtered his ire. "Just too busy to call the friends you sleep with."

Her backbone straightened. "I don't have friends I sleep with."

"Just enemies?"

That was just about enough. Keeping her voice neutral yet civil, she said, "If you came here to be rude to me, then I'd like to invite you to leave."

"I came here to say something to you, Heidi." He

was pacing now and she didn't press. Just waited for him to speak. And to leave for the last time.

"Here's the deal. There was one thing I failed to say the weekend of the reunion. One thing I have to get off my chest whether or not it makes any difference to you."

Shoving the guest chair away from the desk, he slapped his palms on the cherry wood and leaned forward. "I love you. I have probably loved you longer than I know. But what I feel isn't the issue."

He loved her? He loved her? Oh God! He loved her! Her knuckles were white from the strain of keeping her hands to herself, but she found her voice to calmly ask, "What *is* the issue, then?"

"Your refusal to get over the assault." The bully straightened and settled crossed arms over his chest. "Yeah, we talked about it. Yeah, you apologized. But you just won't let it go. Heidi, baby. You've got to let it go."

"I have no idea what you're talking about," she lied, her mouth drawn tight. She really didn't want to hear any of this.

Ben ignored her. "I've spent a lot of time in the last month thinking about you, trying to figure out why you haven't called. And it's the only thing that makes sense. You're all twisted up over this and it's going to destroy you."

She lifted one shoulder. "Destructive acts destroy, Ben. The nature of the beast. What I've spent a lot of time thinking about is how you managed to keep the cops out of it."

"Hell—" he gestured with one wild hand "—I told my folks I didn't remember who'd hit me. That I didn't remember anything that had happened after the bell rang that day. They knew my memory loss was bogus, but I wasn't going to turn you in."

"What!" This was all so unreal! That he'd done that to protect her? She pressed the flat of her palm to her forehead, felt the staccato pulse in her wrist at the bridge of her nose. Then... She jerked her head back up, used her hand as a stop sign. "Wait, wait. You didn't have to turn me in. Everyone knew it was me!"

"Sure. The rumors flew. But I never said a word. And there weren't any witnesses. I wasn't going to ruin what was left of your life by admitting to anything. I had that much sense left."

"No. You'd been knocked senseless."

"You were my friend, Heidi. I'd seen where you lived. The shit you'd survived. And I knew that, given a chance, you'd make a hell of a lawyer. So I forgave you and took the blame.

"But I've gotten over being forgiving. I won't forgive you for holding on to this and ruining the rest of your life. I've been waiting fifteen years for you to get over it. I'm tired of waiting. I love you too much for that."

And then he turned and walked out of her life, leaving Heidi to face the pathetic truth. She was about to lose the best thing she had ever known, and all because she was too much of a snob to admit she was wrong.

She looked out the window again, saw Ben crossing the parking lot. She grabbed up a pen, a white linen gold-embossed notecard and ran out the door of her office, bypassing Georgia's gaping mouth with nothing but a, "Have Annette hold my calls."

BEN HAD SAID what he'd come to say. Now the rest was up to Heidi. Even if he hadn't loved her, he couldn't in all good conscience watch a friend self-destruct.

He'd already given her time. His generous mood was waning. If he didn't hear from her in a week, or two, a month at the outside, well...that would be the end of that.

So sue him that he wasn't the enabling type.

When he heard running footsteps on the concrete behind him, he didn't turn. He kept walking because he couldn't be sure who the feet belonged to and he didn't want to look like a fool if she was watching him from her office window.

But she wasn't. She was there, flushed and out of breath and disheveled.

"Here." She shoved a piece of paper into his face.

He eyed it warily. "What is it?"

"Just take it," she insisted, shaking it his direction.

He took it. And smiled. And felt the earth lift from his shoulders.

It was a check. Well, sort of a check. Nothing he could cash in a bank, but then, this check he wouldn't need to.

Still, he had to hear the words. "Are you sure?"

She nodded. "I love you, Ben."

He swept her up in his arms, business suit and low-heeled pumps and classy hairdo and all. He'd parked at the edge of a cycling trail, and now kissed her all the way there. Then he lowered her to the ground and opened the door of his truck.

"Let's go."

She climbed in and he followed, the slip of paper

floating from his hand to the ground behind him, landing beneath the landscaped hedges next to a discarded bicycle chain.

So it was only the birds who nested in the hedge and the squirrels that buried pecans in the loose dirt beneath who read what Heidi had written.

Pay to the order of: Ben Tannen
Amount: My love and the rest of my life.
Signed: The Mighty Heidi Malone.

Epilogue

"This has got to be the screwiest wedding party in the history of wedding parties."

Standing inside the small foyer of the Stonebridge Community Church, Quentin used the gilded lobby mirror to adjust the knot of his tie. He spoke to the other man's reflection.

"We're in a church. We're not underwater or falling through the air or on a baseball field or wearing water skis. Be thankful for the little things."

"What about the big things? Like the fact that I'm not old enough to be Heidi's father." Grumbling, Randy elbowed his way in front of the mirror to check the cut of his hair.

"Age is no big deal. You want big? Try this on for size." Quentin pushed Randy back out of his way. "I'm not female enough to be Heidi's maid of honor."

"Man of honor." Randy gave up and checked his reflection from over Quentin's shoulder. "I heard her make the distinction."

"All I can say is that this is the end of The Deck as far as I'm concerned." Quentin fought loose the tie until the ends dangled free. "I've gone way above and beyond my duties as queen."

Sunlight filled the small vestibule as Jack pulled open the church's front door. Smiling widely, sunglasses in place, he opened his arms. "Men! How is the *MaidMan of Honor* and the *Phony Father of the Bride?*"

Quentin returned to his tie and the mirror. "Laugh all you want, Montgomery. You'll look back on this day with nothing but generic best man memories. I'll look back and remember..." he groaned, abandoned the tie "...how good I looked in plum?"

"Here, here, now. Let me help you with that." Mrs. Jones scurried into the foyer from the church's nursery where she'd been fine-tuning the bride.

She turned her skills on Quentin. With quick work and nimble fingers, she adjusted his tie. Standing back, she clasped her hands to her mouth and surveyed her handiwork. "You look like a—"

"A queen?" Randy supplied over her right shoulder.

Cutting her eyes that direction, she reached back and smacked him on the arm. "Stop that nonsense. He looks like a vision. A pure vision."

"A vision of what?" Quentin glanced down at his pants of dark purple linen, his lavender shirt, his plum silk tie. He couldn't decide if this vision was fruit or flower, even though Heidi had assured him the colors were androgynously unisex.

Androgynous had never been a look he'd gone for. This *maidman* business was for the birds. But for Heidi...

Mrs. Jones hooked her arm through Quentin's and shouldered Randy completely out of the picture as she stared at their mirrored images. She smiled widely, beamed even, and the next minute shook her finger in his face. "You have my Ben's ring?"

Quentin pulled the braided gold band from his shirt pocket. "Right here."

"What about you?" Mrs. Jones meant business when she glanced at Jack.

"Yes, ma'am." Jack pushed his one elbow off the guestbook stand and flashed Heidi's ring stuck tight to the end of his little finger.

"I don't know, Mrs. Jones," Randy said. He shook his head, working at a straight face. "That ring doesn't look very secure there to me."

Mrs. Jones narrowed her eyes and headed toward Jack. "Let me see."

"Trust me. It's safe." Jack slung his hand. The ring didn't even budge. "It's so safe that I'm close to losing the use of this finger for the rest of my life."

"Well, let's get some soap and water before we run out of time and I pull out my sewing shears." Grabbing him by the lapel, Mrs. Jones headed toward the men's room.

Footsteps clicked on the foyer's linoleum flooring. "Soap and water? Why, Mrs. Jones. Is one of these boys too dirty for church?"

Quentin and Randy and Jack all turned at the new female voice. One at a time three mouths opened, three tongues dragged the floor, and three men stood dumbstruck at the figure standing in the doorway to the church nursery.

Her dress was two layers, the top a sheer gown flowing to her knees in colors from lavender to plum, her patent leather alligator pumps dyed-to-match. But it was the layer of fabric clinging to her body causing the case of triple drop-jaw.

The narrow sheath of a deep violet hue outlined

every voluptuous curve of a very voluptuous body. She was tall, all legs and curves and a wild mane of hair. Her lips and nails were deep wine, her skin café latte.

Quentin was the first to recover. "Georgia?"

Georgia nodded, pressed an index finger to her chin. She glided into the foyer proper with a walk and a smile that didn't belong in a church. "My guess would be Quentin."

Randy stepped between the two before Quentin could reply. "Randy, here. Jack, there. He's the one needing to be cleansed."

"Hello, Randy. Jack." Georgia acknowledged both men, then turned to Quentin. "I admire your work. A lot."

He accepted the compliment with a small bow. "You work with Heidi, so I know I admire yours."

Georgia laughed, a deep chesty laugh that had three pair of male eyeballs popping out of three male heads. Even Jack, who received a resounding, "Get your behind back in here," from Mrs. Jones, stuck his head through the men's room door at the sound.

"Well, I am so pleased to meet all you boys." Georgia sauntered farther into the foyer. "I've been hearing a lot of stories for a lot of years. It's nice to put names to faces and, uh, to the rest of you all."

"Dang it, Georgia. Leave my men alone."

Heidi stood in the nursery doorway and in that moment no other woman existed for the two men in the foyer and the one toweling his hands dry as he left the men's room with the ring as secure in his pocket as it had been on his finger.

She'd forgone traditional bridal wear for a drop-waisted slip with a handkerchief hem on an ankle-length skirt of crinkled ivory. The accompanying jacket tied in front with satin ribbons, and antique lace edged the placket, the hem and the cuffs.

She wore her hair up and pearls around her neck and a sheer shoulder-length veil that fell from a crown of ivory roses. Her shoes were old-fashioned and her stockings sheer cream and the effect rendered her audience breathless.

Georgia was the first to speak. With a hand propped on one hip, she clicked her tongue. "Mmmm. I have looked good in my time but I have never looked like I was spun from heaven's sugar."

Randy crossed the foyer. He took hold of Heidi's left hand and looked her over. "She's right. You are gorgeous."

"Not gorgeous." Jack shook his head. "Gorgeous doesn't get this good. This is..." He gestured with an encompassing motion. "This is..."

"Delicious." Quentin slowly nodded. "And believe me. In my business? I know delicious."

Heidi blushed. Just like a bride was supposed to. "You're not dog food yourself. Any of you."

"Well, I should certainly say we are not." Mrs. Jones moved back to the mirror, adjusted her clerical collar above her white robe. "And just wait until you see that groom. My, my, my. If he looked any sharper, Mr. Jones might indeed have a reason to stick even closer to my side."

Heidi and the others laughed. Mrs. Jones turned toward the nursery doorway, crossed toward the glowing bride and took hold of both Heidi's hands. "You are the best thing that could've ever happened to that Ben Tannen. Don't you let him forget it for a minute."

"How could he? With you and me both there to remind him?" Overwhelmed by the fierceness of the older woman's loyalty, Heidi enveloped her in a hug. She smelled like cinnamon and apples and fresh country air and home, and Heidi's throat swelled for what she knew would not be the only time today.

Blinking back tears threatening to ruin hours' worth of artful makeup application, Heidi turned to the rest of her friends. Friends whom she'd loved for years. Friends who knew what this day, what this man, what this marriage meant.

Friends who were the blessings of her life. "I can't imagine a more perfect day. To have all of you here?" She sobbed once, laughed, blinked harder. "Thank you all. For being here. For being a part of this."

"We wouldn't have missed this day for the world." Georgia came forward and took her turn. "That nice little bonus in my paycheck guaranteed it."

Heidi batted at Georgia's shoulder. "You are about to be uninvited, without a partner and, if I can think of a way to manage it, disbarred."

"Uh-uh-uh." Georgia shook one finger. "You forget. I know too many of your secrets."

And Heidi trumped with, "I don't have any more secrets, remember?"

"Hmm. I guess you're right. Well, then, I'll see you in church." Georgia leaned forward to add in a whisper, "I love you, Heidi," then turned away before both their makeup was a lost cause.

Heidi held out a hand to Jack before Mrs. Jones dragged him away. "I'm glad you're here for Ben."

Jack blew off her gratitude. "It's more like I'm here because of him. But you're welcome." He held the fingers of both her hands, raised them to his lips, then leaned forward and planted his mouth on hers.

"Jack!" she cried, after pulling away. "My lipstick!"

The shrug of his shoulder wasn't the least bit apologetic. "Just getting in the best man's kiss while the groom's not around to knock the crap outta me."

"He's gonna have to get in line behind me if you don't start acting more like a best man and less like a man about town." Mrs. Jones grabbed Jack by the elbow and hauled him to the auditorium door. "You and me have business at the pulpit. We'll see the rest of you in church."

The group in the foyer laughed as the one-hundred-ten-pound Mrs. Jones bulldozed the big bad Jack down the aisle toward the anteroom where Ben would be waiting.

Ben. Oh, Ben. Heidi sighed, suppressed a shiver and turned to Quentin waiting to take his place behind Georgia where she stood at the door. "You look wonderful."

He grimaced, fluttered the ends of his tie with long fingers. "Yeah. For a maid."

His misery was just so puppy-dog cute that she had a hard time keeping a straight face. "You make a wonderful maid, Quentin."

He grimaced. "Don't let my publicist hear you say that. He's already given me grief for telling a reporter that I went through high school as The Queen."

Heidi reached up to straighten his tie and couldn't help but tease. "Is that really such a bad thing?"

"It wouldn't be." There was that Brad Pitt brow again. "If I didn't love women so much."

"And women love you, too. Especially this woman." Heidi wrapped her arms around his waist and held him close.

He returned the embrace. "Ah, Heidi. I couldn't be any happier for you. Or for Ben. I could be happier for me, though. Especially if you'd tell me more about Georgia."

With a gasp of exasperation, Heidi pushed him away. "Hey. Me, me, me. Pay attention to me. This is my day to shine, remember?"

She cut a sly look to her single bridesmaid dressed in violet and chiffon, then glanced back at Quentin. Matchmaking wheels began to whir. "Besides, Georgia would eat you alive."

"I was hoping you'd say that." And with a wink he moved away to take his place behind the object of his affection.

Heidi rolled her eyes and walked toward her two attendants, linking her arm through Randy's when he offered. She took a deep breath. "Ready?"

"One question."

"Shoot."

Patting her hand where it lay on his arm, he puffed out his chest, lowered his voice, and asked, "As father of the bride, when do I get to sit down with the groom and have my little talk?"

"Talk?"

Randy nodded with all seriousness. "Young boys these days. Selfish punks. Don't know how to treat a girl."

"Ah. That talk. Well, I think *never* would be the perfect time for that," she answered, patting the hand still resting on hers then tweaking his ear.

"Yeowch! Okay, okay. I'll just keep my mouth shut." He pretended to rub the sting from his ear. "You two kids deserve each other, you know that?"

The smile that spread over her face came from a place deep in her heart that no one but Ben Tannen had been able to find. A place even she hadn't known existed. "Yes. We do."

She needed a moment, just a moment alone. She pulled her arm from Randy's. He dropped a kiss on her cheek, gave her a wink and moved to wait with Georgia and Quentin.

Heidi smiled at the three of them and opened the church's front door. Walking out onto the first stone step, she stood in the midmorning sun and breathed deep of the fresh clean country air.

The only cars in the small gravel parking lot belonged to the friends inside. Her friends and Ben's. No one else. This day was an intimate celebration, which the guest list reflected.

She'd almost declined to attend the reunion. What an ironic twist of fate if she had. No renewing old friendships, no rekindling of old flames. No reminiscing, no remembering, no regurgitating.

She laughed to herself and even her laugh sounded watery and weak. High emotion ruled the moment, plucking at the strings of her heart. And she wanted to feel it all.

To capture every nuance of what it meant to be surrounded by so much love. To have found this place of contentment, of belonging. To know this man.

Heidi Tannen. Mrs. Ben Tannen. A sob of joy spilled forth.

Every road of her life's journey had been leading to today and the years ahead waiting to unfold. She'd be entering them rich in friendships, as the wife of the man she'd loved for most of her life. And would love for all the years that remained.

"Heidi? Sweetie?"

Heidi turned at Georgia's voice.

"Unless you're thinking of hitting the road, it's time to face the music."

It was then through the open door that Heidi heard the sax. "The Bridal March" played in the low sexy drawn-out tones of an alto's voice. Ben had surprised her with this. He'd told her he'd take care of the music and this is what he had done.

The sun was shining, the grass was green and suddenly she couldn't wait for the rest of her life.

Mr. Jones was securing the auditorium door as Heidi entered the foyer. He gave her a wink, she answered with a warm smile as she returned her hand to the crook of Randy's elbow. A deep breath later, she nodded at Georgia who started down the aisle.

Quentin followed, adding a good-natured roll of his eyes at the indignity of it all. Heidi barely suppressed a chuckle. And then she was up, squeezing Randy's arm as they started toward the front of the church and the man who drew her gaze.

The rogue wore a tender smile and his eyes glistened as he followed her progress. Heidi knew nothing but Ben and her heart, and the days that waited for their love and laughter.

He was her husband. She was his wife. This ceremony was only a ceremony.

The sax drifted away as she and Randy passed the last pew and stopped. Mrs. Jones cleared her throat and glanced from Heidi to Ben. "Who gives this woman to be married to this man?"

Heidi's grin reached from ear to ear when Ben winked and smiled.

And while the two lovers came together as one, Quentin and Randy and Jack answered, "We do."

 HARLEQUIN®

Makes any time special ™

In celebration of Harlequin®'s golden anniversary

Enter to win a *dream!* You could win:

- A luxurious trip for two to
  The Renaissance Cottonwoods Resort
  in Scottsdale, Arizona, or

- A bouquet of flowers once a week for a year
  from **FTD**, or

- A $500 shopping spree, or

- A fabulous bath & body gift basket, including
  K-tel's *Candlelight and Romance* 5-CD set.

Look for **WIN A DREAM** flash on
specially marked Harlequin® titles by
Penny Jordan, Dallas Schulze,
Anne Stuart and Kristine Rolofson
in October 1999*.

RENAISSANCE.
COTTONWOODS RESORT
SCOTTSDALE, ARIZONA

FTD

K·TEL

*No purchase necessary—for contest details send a self-addressed envelope to
Harlequin Makes Any Time Special Contest, P.O. Box 9069, Buffalo, NY, 14269-9069
(include contest name on self-addressed envelope). Contest ends December 31, 1999.
Open to U.S. and Canadian residents who are 18 or over. Void where prohibited.

PHMATS-GR

"This book is DYNAMITE!"
—Kristine Rolofson

"A riveting page turner..."
—Joan Elliott Pickart

"Enough twists and turns to keep everyone
guessing... What a ride!"
—Jule McBride

See what all your favorite authors
are talking about.

Coming October 1999 to a retail store near you.